SNOBS, DOGS AND SCOBIES

SNOBS, DOGS AND SCOBIES

ELIZABETH O'HARA

Little Island

SNOBS, DOGS AND SCOBIES
Published 2011
by Little Island
128 Lower Baggot Street
Dublin 2
Ireland

www.littleisland.ie

First published in Irish as *Hurlamaboc* by Cois Life in Dublin in 2006

Copyright © Éilís Ní Dhuibhne 2006
English translation copyright © Elizabeth O'Hara 2011

The author has asserted her moral rights.

ISBN 978-1-908195-04-3

British Library Cataloguing Data. A CIP catalogue record for this book is
available from the British Library.

Book design by Someday

Printed in Poland by Drukarnia Skleniarz

Little Island received financial assistance from
The Arts Council (An Chomhairle Ealaíon), Dublin, Ireland.

10 9 8 7 6 5 4 3 2 1

To Ailbhe

AWARDS

Snobs, Dogs and Scobies was first published in Irish as *Hurlamaboc* (Cois Life, 2006)

Winner of a Bisto Merit Award 2007

Duais Oireachtais 2006

Shortlisted for Irish Book of the Year 2006

ABOUT THE AUTHOR

Elizabeth O'Hara is the pen name of Éilís Ní Dhuibhne, a well-known author.

She has written many books for young people in Irish and English. She has won the Bisto Book of the Year Award and two Bisto Merit Awards. *Hurlamaboc* (Cois Life) won a Bisto award and was selected for the IBBY Honour List. Her latest book *as Gaeilge* for young people is *Dordán* (Cois Life, 2011).

Elizabeth O'Hara lives in County Dublin. She is a member of Aosdána.

1.

THE BLOOM YEARS

RUÁN

It was Lísín's twentieth wedding anniversary. (And Pól's.)

They were going to celebrate with a big party in a week's time. The whole family was looking forward to it. That's what they said, anyway.

'It'll be awesome,' said Cú, the younger son. His name was Cúán, but they called him Cú for short. He was thirteen.

'Yeah, it's going to be cool,' said Ruán, the older son, who was eighteen. He didn't believe the party would be cool; he knew it would be crap. But he had learnt that it was a good idea to tell his mother exactly what she wanted to hear. Everybody else did.

And Lísín was happy. She knew the day would be wonderful, the celebration fantastic, the party amazing, just as it should be. Her life was a triumph, a complete and utter success. When she'd married Pól he was just an immature weed of a boy without a single achievement to his name and with an abysmal lack of ambition. He was working in a shop at the time of the engagement – a shop boy is what he was. It was she, Lísín, who had spotted the potential in that ignorant youth. And look at him now: a wealthy, learned scion of society, respected by all. A big shot. A fine house, a family of sons, one more handsome and clever than the next.

Well, there were only two sons. Still, they had plenty to celebrate.

As far as the actual party was concerned, everything was under control: Lísín had ordered wine and glasses at the wine shop; the big fridge in the kitchen was stuffed with pies and sausages and salmon and homemade breads of every conceivable kind. She had rented a second refrigerator – you can do that; not many people know it but Lísín did; that's the kind of person she was – and that fridge, out in the garage, was also filled with good things to eat. Sweet stuff, mostly, and some things which were not sweet but wouldn't fit into Fridge Number One.

If the day was fine, they would hold the party out in the garden; the neighbours had promised to lend Lísín extra chairs and tables. And if it was a bad day it didn't matter one bit: the house was more than big

enough for all the guests. And it was pristine, everything neat and clean and tidy. Fresh paint on the
walls, gleaming polish on the floors, flowers in all
the vases.

Perfect, as this house always was. The Allbright
house. Lísín's.

Lísín was an exemplary housewife. Or home-
maker, as she preferred to be called. The house was
always neat and beautiful, and Lísín, too, was always
neat and beautiful. In general it is either one thing
or the other, but not in Lísín's case.

'Who'd believe that your mum was twenty years
married,' said Mr Smith, one of the neighbours, to
Ruán when he came around to the front door to
accept the invitation to the party. 'Or that she could
have a big lump of a fellow like you for a son. She
looks like a slip of a girl herself.'

'Yeah,' agreed Ruán without enthusiasm. But
Mr Smith was right. Lísín did look young. She still
looked OK, for a mother. Slim, with long, blonde
hair. Well, all the mothers on this road, Ashfield
Avenue, had long, blonde hair. It was a blonde
road, although the men were dark: they had black
or brown hair or, more often, grey. But there was
not a single grey-haired woman on the road, and,
more remarkable still, only one brunette: Eileen,
Emma Murphy's mother, whose hair was black.
But Eileen was strange in many other ways.
Nobody really knew how she had managed to get
a house on this road.

All the other women had fair hair, and they were attractive and trendy. That's how it was. There were high standards on the road as far as these matters were concerned; no woman would dream of going outside without her make-up on or decent clothes. Even when they were running out with the wheelie bins they wore lovely dressing gowns, and their hair would be nicely brushed so that the dustbin men would understand that they were good people, even if they couldn't always manage to get up in time to put out the bin.

All the women were like that. But Lísín had something extra, an edge on them. She was more fashionable and better dressed and more blonde than anyone else. In short, she was perfect.

Ruán sighed, thinking about her. He loved his mother. He didn't understand why she irritated him all the time when all she gave him was praise and encouragement.

'I'll tell her you're coming,' he said to Mr Smith. 'She'll be delighted.' And he shut the door rather hurriedly. There was something about Mr Smith that upset him. He was friendly and cheerful and he usually had a joke or two. But he had the sharp eyes that schoolteachers have. Even at the door, those eyes were staring at Ruán, boring into him as if they were doing an X-ray, taking photographs of everything that was on his mind and hidden in his heart.

4

Slim, pretty, cheerful. A great housewife, and at the same time active in many other spheres. That was Lísín. She didn't have a job. Why would she? Pól was doing well, thanks to her: he was a university lecturer in business studies, but that was the source of his status, not, of course, of his money. He played the stock market on the Internet. He was canny and sensible and knowledgeable about finance, and had amassed considerable wealth at this stage. And it was all invested wisely in areas where hardly any tax was collected. He owned houses and apartments as well, at home and here and there around the continent, and he collected rents from all of them.

Why would Lísín go out to work? There was no need whatsoever for it. So she stayed at home. But she kept herself busy. She was a member of several organisations and clubs: clubs that read books, clubs that did charitable work for poor people, clubs that organised lectures on local history and geography and literature, and on how to design a garden that's nicer than your neighbours' or how to decorate your house so that everyone will be sick with envy. And if that wasn't enough, Lísín went to language classes: Spanish, Russian, Chinese, Japanese – she'd taken courses on all of them. And on top of all that she was keenly interested in film and drama. No, she was never idle, and she had made an interesting woman of herself, one who could talk about any subject under the sun.

Honestly.

2.

LÍSÍN'S CHOICE

RUÁN

What about Ruán?

The hero. The main protagonist of this story.

There's not much to say about him.

He was going to do his Leaving Certificate in a month's time. Like about sixty thousand other people. Nothing very remarkable about that.

He was a good student. Not surprisingly. It was difficult to avoid being a good student in the Allbright house, where every facility was laid on, every encouragement given. Never too much pressure and never too little. So, inevitably, Ruán was competent at everything he undertook.

But he had one unusual trait: his favourite subject was not maths or economics or science, but art.

That's what he loved. And his ambition was to get a place in the National College of Art and Design and become a painter.

But he hadn't applied to art school. On his CAO form, the first preference he filled in was business studies. The second was computer science and engineering was third.

He would have liked to put art down first, but he didn't have a chance of getting into NCAD, so there was no point. That's what Lísín told him.

'You won't get it,' she said. 'But put it down anyway. Give yourself a chance. Preparing the portfolio will take a huge amount of time and effort, and it will affect your other studies, but do it if it's what you really want.'

Ruán attempted to get the portfolio together, but he gave up after a while and in the end he didn't bother applying for art at all.

Lísín was very pleased with him.

'It's not a real qualification,' she said. 'You have to have a career, and what sort of a career is art? A passport to poverty.'

They were not her exact words. Lísín was far too thoughtful and sensible to make any harsh remarks about anything, especially anything relating to art.

Art! She was constantly reminding people that she admired art more than anything: pictures and books and plays and films. She loved them all. She went to the opera whenever an opera was on in town, and she listened to Lyric FM when she was driving around in her Jeep. Ten paintings by young Irish artists were hanging on the walls of the house. These were investments, of course. Lísín watched and liked nothing better than to learn that the reputation of one of her artists was growing, and with it the value of the pictures on her sitting-room wall. But she loved those pictures for their own sakes. Really loved them. Just as she loved arthouse film. She kept her membership of the Irish Film Institute in Temple Bar renewed, and she even went to films there occasionally – well, once a year at the very least. Yes, she loved art and creativity and her admiration for artists knew no bounds.

But it was a risky proposition to be a professional artist.

How much more sensible to get a proper career for yourself as a businessman, or something in computers, or even a teacher, like Pól. Of course Pól was not just a teacher: he was a lecturer, and he'd be a professor soon if all went well. There *is* a difference.

If you were passionate about art you'd keep it up anyway. As a pastime. You could do it in your spare time, at the weekend, or during the holidays if you became a teacher. Or a lecturer. Or a professor.

Of course, Lísín was right. As usual.

Ruán was hoping to get a place on BESS – business, economics and social sciences. He'd like to go to Trinity, and Lísín would like that too. It was such an old university, and so charming, and it always came out at the top of the *Sunday Times* league table. She just loved the cobblestones and the bell tower – the Campanile. As well as that, it was close to the Dart station and not far from the Luas.

The big problem with University College Dublin – UCD – was that it was so hard to get to the damned place, Lísín said. Oh yes, the points were low, for the most part – another big disadvantage about UCD, if you were clever like Ruán. Why would a boy like Ruán want to belong to a club any nitwit with a couple of Bs and Cs could get into? Yes, it was easy – all too easy – to get to UCD, in that sense, the points sense. But getting there physically was another matter entirely. The Dart doesn't go to UCD, nor the Luas. Nothing goes there except the number ten bus, which is no use at all to people living in the Dun Laoghaire-Rathdown district. For them, Trinity is the only college that makes any sense.

Lísín kept up the pressure on Ruán at home while, at school, the teachers took over. Press, press, press, from morning to night.

'Four hours of study after school. Six on Saturday. Take notes. Write down important concepts on index cards. They will be easy to consult just before the examination. Take a day off on Sundays. Take frequent breaks. Get enough fresh air and exercise. Go for a swim. Play football …'

There was no end to the stream of advice. How would you possibly have time to go swimming, to play football, if you were studying for four hours every evening after getting home from school at five o'clock? Go swimming in the middle of the night, is that what they meant? Go off for a bracing game of football at the dawning of the day?

'I'm getting nothing done,' said Mícheál, Ruán's schoolfriend, on the train one day. He went to school on the Dart, like Ruán. He lived in a neighbouring suburb, at the station next to Ruán's. 'I'll probably fail, but who cares?'

'Yeah, yeah,' said Ruán. He'd heard that spiel many times. He wasn't sure if Mícheál really believed he was doing no work or if he was well aware that he was lying through his teeth. He always got great marks although he claimed to do no work at all. Maybe he was a genius. Not like Ruán, who had to work and study his ass off to get any sort of decent result.

Emma Murphy was also on the train. Ruán didn't spot her until he was getting off. Too late to escape.

'Hi, Ruán,' she said. She was the same age as he. Dressed in the uniform of Mulberry Manor, a convent school located in a castle at the foot of the hill. She was a dog, according to Mícheál and the other guys. Ruán thought she looked OK. Nice, even. She was fair-haired and had a friendly face, but she was too fat, in Mícheál's estimation. Her skin was a soft creamy colour, and she reminded Ruán of vanilla soufflés. However, it didn't matter what she reminded *him* of; being seen in her company was terrible for his image.

'Hi,' he said, very quietly.

He didn't utter another syllable until the Dart had pulled out of the station and he was sure that Mícheál couldn't see him any more.

Then he started a conversation.

'How's life?'

'It's OK,' she smiled. She was always cheerful. 'I hear you guys are having a big bash on Saturday.'

'Oh, yeah,' said Ruán, without enthusiasm. 'My parents are.'

'My mum is looking forward to it,' said Emma. 'A get together with all the glitterati of Ashfield Avenue!' Emma's folks had split up years ago. Her mum was a single parent. That was one of the things that made her slightly off-kilter on Ashfield Avenue. 'She's even trying to get me to come. When will the invites go out?'

'Don't know,' said Ruán. 'Sure they tell me nothing.' He knew most of them had gone out days ago. 'Anyway, that party will be crap.'

She was surprised and gave a little chuckle.

'It will? How do you mean?'

'Old fogies getting pissed. Yuck! I'm going to make myself scarce on Saturday, I can tell you that.'

'You're not going to be there? At your parents' anniversary party?'

'No way. I mean … no way am I going to be there. But hey, come along anyway. You might enjoy it. If you're completely crazy or something.'

'Well, maybe I will go.'

She had no cop-on. That was a thing with girls. No cop-on. They didn't think fast enough. Never came up with the right retort, didn't get it when you were slagging. Girls were so serious compared to guys.

'No, seriously. Don't bother. I'll be having a real party a few days later.'

'A few days after your mother's party?'

It was annoying the way she repeated what he'd just said. Like an echo. He always hated it when people did that.

'Yes. With the leftovers. If there are any leftovers. That shower would drink the water from the toilet.'

She laughed at that. They were coming round the corner of their road now. Some of the little kids out playing in the shade of the chestnut trees said hello to Emma.

'My mum has ordered a hundred bottles of wine though. So there might be one or two bottles left over after they've drunk themselves comatose.'

She laughed again.

That was one good thing about her: she thought he was funny. Usually when he tried to say something funny to Mícheál and the guys they sighed loudly and told him to shut up.

That was that. Now he'd have to organise a party. And he hadn't a clue how to do it. But he had ten days to think about the problem. So he put it on the long finger, planning to think about it later, when the time was right. Then he forgot all about it, which is what Ruán tended to do with problems. He banished them from his mind.

Emma was at the station again a few days later, on her way to school. Ruán didn't want to start talking to her because there was a good chance that Mícheál would be on the next train in, and he'd slag Ruán to death if he caught him chatting to a dog like Emma. But he couldn't avoid saying hello to her.

All Emma did in response, however, was to incline her head ever so slightly. She did not smile. In fact, she looked unfriendly.

That startled him.

What was going on?

Now he wanted to have a chat with her. He didn't give a damn about Mícheál's opinion, or anyone else's.

Instead of going to the end of the queue, as he had intended to do initially, he went and stood right beside Emma. It was OK to jump the queue at the Dart station. There never was a proper queue there anyway. When the train came, everyone rushed for it, en masse. It wasn't orderly like the queues at the bus stop; it was a free for all. Survival of the fittest: that was the motto of the Dart.

'So, how's it going?' he asked nicely.

'OK,' she said. But her voice was cold.

What the hell could he say now? Suddenly his mind was blank and he couldn't think of a thing. The weather? That's what his parents did when they couldn't think of anything interesting to say: they started talking about the weather. But that was so unbelievably stupid.

'It's a nice day, isn't it?' he said.

This time she didn't even reply. Maybe she shared his opinion regarding small talk about the weather.

He looked carefully at her. By now it was clear that something was bothering her. But what? He couldn't have done anything to upset her. He hadn't laid eyes on her for three days or more.

He racked his brains, hunting for something to say.

What was it his dad said when Lísín was in one of her bad moods? Not that they happened very often, since Lísín was Little Mrs Sunshine most of the time.

'Your shoes are nice,' is what he came up with.

She was wearing big black shoes with thick, wedgy soles. Ruán didn't have an opinion about them one way or the other. On the whole, however, these probably would not be his favourite type of female footwear. They were like horse's hooves. A carthorse's.

'*What?*' she said, genuinely astonished.

At least he'd succeeded in breaking her out of that heavy silence.

And at that moment the train came. Emma shoved her way into a carriage full of girls from her school. Ruán followed but he didn't get a seat close to her; he had to stand at the end of the carriage. From that vantage point he kept a close eye on Emma and the rest of them. From time to time they cast furtive glances in his direction. After about ten minutes one of the girls started to giggle. And then they all joined in. Soon they were all breaking their sides laughing.

They made such a racket that everyone in the carriage was annoyed. But nobody more so than Ruán.

They kept glancing at him slyly and then at one another, the way girls do. He got it. He was just a joke. What was wrong with him?

3.

THE GARDEN PARTY

RUÁN

The sun was shining on the day of the party, much to Lísín's gratification.

'The gods are looking after us!' she exclaimed. Lísín did not believe in God but she was always talking about 'the gods', though it wasn't clear which gods she was referring to. She gazed all around the beautiful garden. Maybe the gods were there, lurking in the shrubbery, behind a bush or up a tree? Or, more likely, in the lavender. Lavender was the theme of the garden this year. Two hundred lavender bushes were planted in the corners of the green lawn. They were in bloom just now, conveniently enough, and by mid-afternoon the air would be filled with their delicious fragrance. In the heart of the lawn was a pond with a fountain at its centre, tinkling sweetly like a perpetual piano. The fountain was a recent acquisition. A tiny little pressie Lísín had given herself. She often gave herself a tiny little pressie of that kind.

Ruán and Cú were to spend the morning helping with the preparations for the party. That was the theory, anyway. Cú went off playing football, just as he did every Saturday. Ruán pretended to clean the bathroom for a while but then he slipped off to his own room and spent the morning playing computer games. He should have been studying for the Leaving. It would start in less than a month. But he had a strategy. Which was that he would begin studying seriously after the party. It was important not to start too soon because then there was a risk of burnout. This had happened to a boy in his school last year. A real swot. He had studied too hard all year and when the exam eventually started everything fell apart for him. He went crazy, and he had to go to hospital and spend two months recovering. Ruán didn't want anything like that to happen to him. Therefore he took great care not to study too much. Most of the time, he studied too little. But everything was under control. In a week's time he'd get started, and he would be at his intellectual peak the day the examinations began.

There would be no lunch this Saturday.

'Lunch?' Pól looked at him as if he were a halfwit. 'We've no time for lunch. The visitors will be coming within the hour.'

'When will we have dinner?' he asked then.

'Are you kidding?' said his father. He was un-corking bottles of wine. He had opened ten already and was about to open ten more.

'Is there anything to eat?' Ruán asked finally.

He knew the garage was full of things: salmon, cold meat of every conceivable kind, salad, millions of cream cakes.

'The house is full of food,' said Lísín with a sigh. She looked tired after all the morning's work and it suddenly struck Ruán that his parents had picked a peculiar way of celebrating their wedding anniver-sary. 'Go out to the garage and get something.'

Ruán didn't fancy the food in the garage – he'd prefer chips or pizza. But he wasn't allowed to eat the food he liked. Lísín was always forcing her children to eat healthy food. Well, there'd be a few changes around here next week, Ruán thought, when they went off on their holiday. Pizza every single day. Or Chinese.

He grabbed a few slices of bread from a basket and scoffed them.

Lísín dashed upstairs to dress and put on her make-up, and then the guests started arriving.

In no time the house and garden were thronged. There were fifty or sixty people at least, all chatting at the tops of their voices. Ruán and Cú had to go around filling their glasses with wine. They drank at high speed and it was hard work keeping those glasses topped up. As soon as Ruán had filled the glasses at one end of the garden, the glasses at the other end were empty.

The neighbours were out in force, of course.

Mr Smith with the gimlet eyes and his wife, Maggie. Her eyes were not sharp, but dead. She looked as if she were falling asleep from exhaustion.

'Such a lovely day,' she said.

That's what most of them said. Sometimes they said, 'You've grown so tall I wouldn't have recognised you.' One or two asked him if he was still at school, but most of them had enough sense not to mention anything relating to school or educational matters.

Eileen, Emma's mother, wasn't present. He noticed this after an hour or so.

'Eileen Murphy isn't here,' he said to Lísín. Lísín was on another planet. She knew the party was a great success. Everyone was chatting and drinking and clearly having a good time. It was a triumph. Another feather in her cap, which was already as full of feathers as a turkey farm.

'Isn't she?' she said absently, paying no real attention to his comment. 'Oh well; she'll come later, probably.'

Lísín didn't care about Eileen, Ruán knew. She was of no importance, as a guest or as a neighbour. It would be another matter entirely if Dr Martin failed to turn up, or Colette Ní Mhistéala, who was a TV presenter and a real star on Ashfield Avenue. Or Brian Flanagan, who owned the big house on the corner, the one with the swimming pool and the tennis court, and who was an important business-man in the city, though nobody was quite sure what his business was. Something to do with finance, or insurance, or houses and property, or a mixture of all those things: it made him very rich, whatever it was, and they were afraid he'd move away to an even better neighbourhood.

He was there, all right, and that was one reason why Lísín was so delighted with herself. She didn't give a damn about Eileen.

The salad and the salmon had been eaten, more or less. The garden was littered with plates and bowls containing leftovers. Quite a few of the guests were drunk. Mr Smith was in the library with Mrs Long, having an earnest discussion about Mrs Smith and the problems he was having in his marriage, thanks to Mrs Smith's low spirits. A small crowd had gath-ered around the TV, where some significant match was in progress. Janet Ní Mhuirí and Betty Boland were washing the dishes.

That's when the horrible moment arrived. Pól stood on a table in the middle of the garden and banged his glass with a spoon.

He was going to give a speech, toasting the guests at the party and toasting Lísín.

Ruán wanted to sink into the ground and disappear. If there was one thing in the world he detested more than any other, it was Pól's speeches. He found them repulsive and he knew that lots of other people considered them over the top.

Pól, however, thought otherwise. He had a high opinion of his own rhetorical skills. He belonged to a society called the Toastmasters. Making speeches was their hobby. They met once a month and gave speeches to one another about their holidays, or childhood adventures, or some other interesting event (right!) that had happened to them. Pól was a diligent Toastmaster and attended every single meeting, always anxious to speechify. Every year he entered a competition for speeches and once he had come sixth in the country, an achievement which gave him great satisfaction. 'Well, I came sixth,' he would say. 'It's not the Olympics. There were over a hundred in for the competition, though, so I'm just a tiny bit chuffed!'

'Ladies and gentlemen!' he was saying from the table top. People were silent, even though they really wanted to keep on chatting about where they were going on their holidays and how clever their children were and how they were going to decorate their houses and gardens.

'We are gathered together on this important occasion!'

You'd think he was outside the GPO, starting an historic revolution, rather than outside his garage, interrupting a good party.

'Twenty years ago, I made the most important decision a man can ever make in his lifetime. Let me put it in context. Fianna Fáil were in government. The Hunger Strikes were in full swing in the Maze Prison in Belfast …'

Yuck! Pól didn't have an ounce of tact. Hunger strike? They had spent the last three hours eating two shoulders of ham and six salmon and drinking nearly a hundred bottles of wine.

People were getting bored with the speech already, after ten seconds. One or two slipped back in to the television, hoping they wouldn't be noticed. But Ruán had his eye on them. Mr Smith was rubbing his foot against Mrs Long's ankle under the table; Ruán noticed that too.

Even Pól noticed that he was losing some of his audience.

He made a few more references to events dating from the historic occasion of his marriage to Lísín, then he thanked everyone for coming to the party and he raised his glass.

Hurrah! yelled everyone.

What do you sing on a day like this? It wasn't somebody's birthday. You couldn't just sing Happy Birthday to You. Happy Anniversary doesn't scan.

'*Sláinte Pól is Lísín, sláinte Pól is Lísín,*' somebody started off. One of the Ó Muircheartaighs. Their kids went to the all-Irish school and they spoke Irish at home all the time. Fanatic *Gaelgeoirs*. Crazy, trying to keep that useless, dead language alive, is what Lísín and a lot of the neighbours thought, although they were careful never to say this in the hearing of any of the Ó Muircheartaighs.

But everyone joined in. If there was one Irish word the people of Ashfield Avenue knew, it was *Sláinte*!

4.

TASTE OF FREEDOM

RUÁN

It was just fantastic to wake up the next morning knowing that the party was over and that Pól and Lísín were on their way to the Eastern World. Or at least to Turkey, where they were going to spend a week extending their celebrations. Cú had been sent off on a little holiday of his own with a friend who lived on the other side of town. A whole week of freedom! And another month till the start of the Leaving Cert! Lísín would be home in good time to oversee the preparations for the exam and to make sure that not one single mark went astray.

The house was as clean as ever. Lísín and Pól had tidied away every trace of the party before they left for the airport. They were up all night cleaning, but they said it didn't matter, they'd sleep on the plane. The flight to Istanbul would take five or six hours. Pól owned an apartment in Istanbul and he needed to look after a few business affairs before they could leave the city and go to a holiday resort on the coast.

Ruán saw them off at about 4 a.m. and then went back to bed and slept until ten o'clock.

Then he got up and immediately started phoning his friends. He'd have his own party tonight. There was no reason to postpone it any longer.

Tomorrow was a school day but he decided not to let that affect him. He wouldn't bother going to school. It occurred to him then that he could take the whole week off. He'd write a note informing the school that he was sick with a cold or flu or some more unusual illness, if he could think of one – he'd have a look on the Internet; he'd find an interesting illness which lasted for a week but wasn't fatal or anything. In any case, he would get a lot more study done at home than in school.

So that was settled.

All he had to do now was sit around and wait for his mates to show up. They all said they'd come and bring their own drinks and whatever else they wanted.

By the time he'd made all the phone calls – about fifteen to his closest pals, but he'd encouraged them to spread the word about the party; he'd have about fifty or sixty people if they all came, he reckoned – the day was half over. Two o'clock.

He went on a little tour of the house. Everything was so clean and neat, it was hard to believe there'd been a big party here the day before. Silence had settled into all the rooms, soothing as cool silk. He sighed happily. How wonderful it was to have the whole house to himself, with nobody around to bother him! As a rule he was like a lodger in this house. Lísín was the boss of everything. It was she who made all the decisions, and Pól backed her up, a yes man, yes to every order and demand, it didn't matter what it was, it didn't matter how silly it was.

Free. He was free! Free, free, free.

But there wasn't as much as one drink left in the house. They drank every single drop, those piss artists. He'd have to buy a couple of bottles himself.

He took the money they'd left him for food and the milkman, and headed off to the Spar in the village.

He bought a dozen cans of the cheapest beer they had in stock, something made in Holland. He and the shop assistant, a guy he half knew, had had an argument about his identity card – Ruán had forgotten to bring ID and this guy had made a big deal of it. In the heel of the hunt he got the beer, but the incident left him in bad form.

As he walked home, lugging the cans, he noticed that it was a fine day again. All the trees that lined the road to the village were in blossom, and the birds were singing their little heads off. Spring was in full sail, without a doubt. Heat in the sun. Maybe folks could sit out in the garden tonight.

'Hi!' He was daydreaming about the party when she said hello. Emma. She was alone, dressed in a tracksuit.

'Oh, hi!' He was glad to see her. She looked really nice in the tracksuit, he thought. 'What are you up to?'

'Going for a run,' she said. 'I'm going to do the mini-marathon.'

'Awesome,' he said, his admiration for her growing. 'Well, that's really cool.'

They stood in the middle of the path. She didn't move on, for some reason.

'Well,' he said again. It was horrible, the way he couldn't come up with a single thing to say when he was with her, he who was usually so chatty and articulate. 'Well … a few of my mates are coming round tonight. Maybe you'd like to drop by, too?'

If Mícheál or anyone asked what a dog like Emma was doing at his party, he'd say she crashed, he decided.

'I don't know,' she said.

He shrugged. 'It's up to you. People will come around eight. It's no big deal. A couple of scoops, music, we'll talk … It'd be really great if you could make it.' He'd been using this formula all day. The words came out of his mouth of their own accord.

'I'll see.' She started getting ready to run off.

Ruán suddenly thought of something.

'Oh! I noticed your mum didn't come to our big bash yesterday,' he said. 'Is she OK?'

'She wasn't invited,' said Emma, and off she ran down the road.

Lísín.

That was so typical. She was a complete and utter snob. Eileen didn't merit an invitation because she was a single parent, because she worked as some sort of secretary in an ordinary office job, because she wasn't rich or important in any way, according to Lísín's standards. Every other neighbour on the road had been at the party.

And she had let on to Ruán that she didn't know why Eileen hadn't turned up.

He wanted to kill his mother.

At the moment she was in an airplane, high above some ocean or mountain range, far, far away. Or maybe on her way to the hotel. But the second she landed he'd be on the phone letting her know exactly what he thought of her. If it were possible to do it by telephone, he'd wreck her holidays for her.

He'd ring again and again and again. If nothing else, he'd run up a massive phone bill for her to pay when she got back from her second honeymoon.

Lísín!

Eight o'clock.

Ruán was watching television, and the clock, and waiting for his friends to arrive.

Half past eight.

Ruán was looking out the window, and at the clock, waiting for his friends to arrive.

Nine o'clock.

Ruán was on the phone. Mícheál had just rung to apologise. He couldn't come after all. His folks didn't want him to go to a party on Sunday night.

'Your parents? Since when did you give a shit about what they thought about anything?'

'That's life,' said Mícheál, hanging up.

Half past nine.

He was on the phone again, ringing people himself now. He called Orla, a friend. Orla was at a party.

'Oh, gosh!' she said. 'Hi, hi. I forgot about your thing. Everybody's around here at Melissa's. Her folks are away somewhere. Why don't you come round?'

'Is Mícheál there by any chance?' said Ruán.

'You bet,' said Orla. 'Mícheál and Brian and Rónán and all the gang. Do you want to talk to him?'

'No, just tell him I called you,' said Ruán. 'Oh, and please tell him he's a total shit and I'll break his head the next time I see him. OK? Talk to you.'

Twenty to ten.

Night had fallen and he couldn't see anything now as he looked out the window. But he sat there anyway, staring out at the black pool of the garden.

They didn't come to his party. They went to Melissa's instead. Melissa was cool. He'd never been cool. That was the problem.

They were a pack of liars, all his so-called friends.

He started to cry. He didn't turn on the light. He just sat there, by the window, weeping.

Ten o'clock.

The phone rang and Ruán jumped. At last!

It was Cú. Ruán's heart sank right back down into his sneakers.

'I forgot my iPod,' Cú said.

Ruán promised he'd give it to him tomorrow although he knew perfectly well he wouldn't do that, because he wouldn't be at school.

He sighed and turned on the TV. *Gone with the Wind*. Crap movie. But he watched it.

Half past ten.

A knock at the door.

Emma.

'Hi,' said Emma. She looked around the hall. 'Is it over already?'

'Oh!' said Ruán. The hall was in darkness. She wouldn't see that he'd been crying. 'No, no. I cancelled it at the last minute. I didn't have your phone number to call you and let you know. I phoned everyone else.'

'Oh, right,' said Emma. 'OK, well, that's a pity. Talk to you.'

'No!' said Ruán quickly. 'No, come in for a minute ...'

She looked quizzically at the dark shadows in the hall. 'Wait!'

He turned on the light. She came in.

'Fancy a beer?' he said. 'I still have all those cans.'

'That'd be nice,' she said.

She sat on the sofa in front of the window. Behind her the trees swayed in the garden like ghosts, black shades whispering and bending in the wind. Ruán could see the moon gleaming like a silver CD in the navy blue sky.

He handed her a can and sat on the other sofa, the white sofa, at right angles to her.

'I'm sorry your mother wasn't invited to the party yesterday,' he said, remembering that he had forgotten to phone Lísín to tell her off. But it didn't matter. He knew he wasn't going to do it now. 'It was just an oversight, I'd say.'

'I don't think so,' said Emma. 'Your mother doesn't like Eileen because she's not married.'

'That's rubbish,' said Ruán. 'She's not like that. Nobody's like that nowadays. All that crap about being married or not married, that doesn't matter any more. Who cares?'

Emma shook her head.

'Some people care. But never mind. It doesn't matter.' She took a slug of beer. 'Your house is beautiful.'

Ruán looked around the room as if he'd never seen it before. It had never crossed his mind that it was either ugly or beautiful. He didn't spend much time here anyway; usually he was in his own room or the den. The walls here were white and there were lots of paintings on them – Lísín's collection. Bright rugs were scattered on the floor and the furniture was covered with light, bright textiles.

'Yeah,' he agreed. 'It's OK.'

'Why did you cancel the party at such short notice?' she asked.

'I felt sick,' said Ruán. 'Then I thought, hey, I've got to get up early for school tomorrow and it really doesn't make sense to have a party tonight.'

He was about to add that he'd have it instead at the end of the week, but he bit the words back and stared at the can of beer he was drinking.

'That was sensible,' she said.

She looked great, he was thinking. Her hair was flowing down her back and she was wearing a pink T-shirt, jeans and nice pink sneakers, not those horrible shoes that looked like hooves. Why did they call her a dog? It was a complete lie.

'My folks are in Turkey,' he said. 'A little extra celebration.'

'They're lucky,' said Emma. 'Your folks. They have it all. They've been married for twenty years, they have a lovely house, they've nice holidays.'

'They have me!' said Ruán.

'Yes,' she nodded. 'Some people have everything, and others ... My mum only owns a little house, and she couldn't go on a big holiday like that. We have to go somewhere with Ryanair, or we go camping in France. That's what we'll do as soon as the holidays come.'

'Well, I think that sounds kind of cool. Camping as soon as school's over. I've no plans at all myself.'

'You're not off to Lanzarote or somewhere like that?'

He shook his head.

He didn't know what he'd do when the Leaving was over. He hadn't given any thought to life after the exams. Some of the gang were going to Majorca but Pól and Lísín wouldn't give him the funds for that. It would be too dangerous, they said. The lads would be drinking all the time and some sort of accident would happen.

There was a knock on the door.

Eleven o'clock. Who could it be?

Mícheál, Rónán, Brian, Orla and about ten others.

'Hey!' they all cried in unison. They were in high spirits. And pissed. They crammed into the hall.

'Hey,' said Emma. 'I thought the party was cancelled?'

'Is there a *party* on here?' Mícheál went over to the CD player and started it. The room filled with the sound of The Sultans of Ping singing 'Where's me jumper!'

The gang thronged into the front room and sat on the yellow sofa, the white sofa and the blue sofa. And on the floor.

Mícheál plonked himself down next to Emma and put his arm around her shoulder.

'Hi, beautiful!' he simpered.

5.

YOUR LOCAL SPAR

COLM

He was already in the Spar at 8 a.m., stacking the shelves with bread. The loaves came at a quarter to and he was there to open the doors and take them inside.

He liked this time of the day. The shop all to himself, the good smell of the newly baked bread, the way he had time to arrange the loaves neatly on the shelves. All the brown loaves side by side, the white pans on another shelf. Brennan's, Nutty Doorsteps, McCambridge's. They stocked thirty different kinds of bread in this small supermarket. Nobody would believe that. Customers would come in and pick one idly, hardly even thinking about it. It would never occur to them that Colm had come in early in the morning to organise all those rolls and pans and turnovers. One was the same as the next, as far as most people were concerned.

Even so, this work gave him intense satisfaction. He loved the silence. He loved putting things in order.

In the shop, everything was organised. There were rules about the time you came in and the time you could leave, rules about what sort of work you should do in the shop, rules about the quarter of an hour break for tea. This was a bone of contention: the tea break wasn't long enough. Everyone complained. 'Back to the slavery!' But they laughed as they gave out. They weren't serious. They were always watching the clock and left the second their shift was over, but while they were at work they were cheerful, good humoured, well mannered. Nobody ever yelled. You couldn't even imagine it happening. Nobody hit anybody. You couldn't imagine that, either. If you raised your hand to a person in the shop they'd call the Gardaí.

Not like at home.

In Colm's house, a lot of screaming went on. Screaming, arguing, fighting. It didn't happen every day but it happened often enough. And often enough the arguing could turn into a real *hurlamaboc*: people hitting one another, breaking things – the cups or the furniture.

It was his father's fault. He was fond of the drop, which meant he drank too much and was probably an alcoholic. Colm understood that, but apparently his father didn't, nor did anyone else at home. Colm's father would be in the pub every Thursday, Friday and Saturday. Then he'd come home and collapse into bed, on lucky days. The other days were the dangerous days, when he was at home with nothing to do but annoy everyone else.

Colm preferred to stay out of the house.

He'd rather be at school. He'd rather be in the shop where he worked nights and every weekend. He'd rather be anywhere else than home.

He pretended he was out with his mates or at school at those times. If his dad found out he had a job, he'd try to grab his wages. Luckily his dad never came into the shop – he didn't do shopping, ever, or any other sort of housework. That was for women or sissies.

Colm gave money to his mother. He had a younger brother at home, and his mother earned only what she got for child-minding a baby belonging to another woman in the neighbourhood. Jacob. When Jacob was in the house, Colm's father behaved himself. He could even be nice. Colette, Jacob's mum, thought Colm's father was a really great guy, friendly and witty, always joking. That's something that disgusted Colm, the way his father changed his spots when outsiders were around. But when they were alone in the house, he was another person entirely. You never knew what would set him off, make him angry: saying something or not saying something, doing something or not doing something. Looking at him or not looking at him.

You just never knew.

When he'd stacked the shelves, Colm opened the front door of the shop. Waiting outside were Molly, Sandra and Niamh and a couple of early customers.

'How are you today?' asked Molly. 'It's lovely and hot out.'

Molly was middle-aged, small and fat, and she had some sort of a speech impediment. She spoke unnaturally slowly. Sometimes people thought she was intellectually impaired, but she was actually very bright, and Colm was extremely fond of her.

'Will you be here all day?' she asked.

He nodded.

'Ah, sure you're as well off.'

Other people were always expressing surprise at the long hours Colm worked and kept encouraging him to take more time off. But Molly didn't pressurise him at all. It was almost as if she understood what motivated his working habits. He knew this couldn't really be the case. She didn't know his family at all, and she lived in another suburb, three miles away from here. She came on the bus.

She was just exceptionally understanding.

Sometimes he thought he'd like to have her for his mother.

His own mother was fine. Her problem was she was married to his father.

He knew Molly wouldn't have made a mistake like that. She had a nice husband – a carpenter. Sometimes he came to the shop to pick her up. He was very quiet and hardly had a word to say, but Colm took this as a good sign.

His own dad always had plenty to say. Lots of *plámás*, designed to make people think he was a really nice guy.

After lunchtime, which he spent in the little tearoom at the back of the shop, Colm went to work in the off-licence, tucked away in a corner of the super-market.

Sunday afternoon. The place was busy enough. People coming and going, buying beer or wine to have with their dinner or to drink sitting out in the garden on a fine day like this.

Colm recognised lots of the customers: people who were regular shoppers in the supermarket, and others who were regulars in the off-licence. They all looked as if they were just ordinary people, not drunkards or alcoholics. But Colm was sceptical about them, knowing his father. If you bumped into him in a shop or on the street, you would never guess what sort of a person he really was – although his nose was turning ever so slightly purple and his face was becoming swollen. But a stranger would pay no attention to those signs.

Colm scrutinised the faces that came to his counter. Occasionally you would get a hint that all was not as it should be. One woman, who was very well dressed and who always had her car key in her hand, she'd place the keys on the counter while she was paying, usually using her Visa card – the whites of her eyes were a pinkish colour. Bloodshot. That was an indication. She had a four-wheel drive, too: he recognised the key.

That sort of thing upset him.

Why did people drink at all? If he ruled the world, he'd ban alcohol completely. It would be universally illegal. He believed that this would happen eventually, some time in the future; the pity was that it hadn't happened yet.

Sometimes a young person would come in trying to buy a six-pack. He had to ask them for ID proving they were over eighteen. It annoyed some of them that he insisted on seeing their ID. The owner of the shop was casual as far as underage drinking was concerned. He was mainly interested in selling his products and didn't really care who bought them.

But Colm was scrupulous in his application of the law and if someone didn't have ID, he sold them nothing.

This afternoon, that guy, Ruán, came into the shop.

Colm recognised him. He knew almost everyone in Rathbeg. The shop was right in the centre of the village and almost everyone came in from time to time. He'd seen Ruán in the shop before, and he knew him well for another reason: they had gone to the same primary school. This happened by accident – of course the children from the council estate where Colm lived didn't go to the same school as the kids from the private houses. The council estate people – the 'scobies', as they were called – had their own primary school in the middle of their estate. There was another primary school and a Protestant school on the side of the hill for the people from the private houses.

But when it was time for Colm to start school, his mother brought him along to the ordinary school and the entrance class was full. She hadn't registered him in time, which was typical of her. The school principal expressed her apologies, but what could she do? She couldn't work miracles.

She telephoned the other primary school, the Catholic one, but they were full also – it was the first of September, the first day of school; of course there were no vacancies. Finally she rang the Protestant school, without much hope, because that was the trendiest school of all in Rathbeg, for Catholics too. But as it happened they had one place. A pupil had been killed in a traffic accident a couple of days before school was due to reopen.

That's how Colm got his place in the most desirable school in Rathbeg, the Protestant school, where Ruán was a pupil. By mistake, filling a dead child's shoes.

Colm and Ruán had sat side by side in the babies' class, and in senior infants as well, and they'd loved one another the way little kids in babies and senior infants do – better than brothers.

But that was years and years ago. By now the Rathbeg class system was functioning properly again; this meant that Ruán was attending a private school far from home, while Colm went to the local comprehensive, the place for folk like him. They didn't meet very often, even though their homes were not far apart, and Ruán was a rare enough customer in the shop.

'Hey, man,' said Ruán. 'How's it going?'

'All right,' said Colm.

'Still working here?' he said.

'Well, that's what my boss thinks,' said Colm. 'You know yourself …'

'Yeah, but it's good to have a job. Are you up for the Leaving this round?'

'Yes, more's the pity,' said Colm.

'Me too. What's the plan for after?'

Colm shrugged.

'Don't know.'

He really did not know. He'd like to get a full-time job here in the shop, or in some other shop, he thought, and a flat of his own. But it would be hard to leave his mother. He couldn't bring himself to think about it.

'No? Well, you're probably right. Wait and see. A gap year would be good. That's most likely what I'll do. I wouldn't mind going to college but I'd like to travel too.' Ruán had no plans to do anything of the kind but he said it to make conversation. 'Round, all round the world.'

They used to watch the Phileas Fogg cartoon when they were kids, and they loved to sing the theme song.

'That'd be sweet,' said Colm, thinking of Phileas Fogg. Round, all round the world. Seemed like a good idea when he was four but he wouldn't want to do it now. He'd be afraid, and he had no interest in travelling. He'd never been abroad in his life. Never even been on a plane. That's something Ruán would be unable to comprehend.

'My folks are in Turkey right now,' said Ruán. 'Wouldn't mind going there. Without them, needless to say.'

'Turkey?' said Colm. He thought he had heard Turkey mentioned earlier today on the news, but he hadn't paid much attention to what the story was about. 'I guess it's very nice over there.'

'Anyway,' said Ruán. 'I'd best leave you to it. Back to work.' There was nobody else in the shop and there was no work to be done. People just said these things. 'So, let me see now. I'll have this lot.' He put two six packs down on the counter.

'OK,' said Colm. 'But I need to see something that confirms you're over eighteen.' He jerked his head at the notice:

IF YOU ARE LUCKY ENOUGH TO LOOK YOUNGER THAN EIGHTEEN, WE WILL HAVE TO DEMAND IDENTIFICATION.

'What, man?' Ruán laughed. 'You were in babies with me.'

'I know. But I need to be sure. You could be seventeen.'

'I could be but I'm not. I'm eighteen.' He laughed again. 'Honest to God! Cross my heart and hope to die!'

'Do you have any ID? Anything? Even a bus pass?'

'No,' said Ruán.

'Well, then I can't sell you these.'

'This is unbelievable!' said Ruán. 'I'll waste the best part of an hour going home for ID and coming back here again. Fuck's sake, man, I really am eighteen!'

Colm shook his head.

'I'm sorry; it's the rule.'

Ruán shook his head too and smiled.

'OK. OK. I get it. Rules. Come to my party tonight anyway, if you feel like it,' said Ruán. 'You know where I live.'

'Thanks,' said Colm, taken aback. 'Yeah, sure, I know where you live.'

He'd gone to a few birthday parties there when he was five or six. But this was the first invitation he'd received since then.

He'd be working here till eleven o'clock, and he didn't think he'd be up to any party after that. It was obvious that Ruán's invitation was less than heartfelt. All the same he was pleased to have been invited. People very seldom invited him to a party, or to anything else. He was always working and he wasn't one bit popular.

He looked at Ruán.

'OK. I know you must be eighteen,' he said. '*I'm eighteeen.*'

And, against all his principles, he sold Ruán the beer.

6.

HURLAMABOC

COLM

Colm went home when the shop shut at eleven o'clock.

His house was close to the village, and the estate where he lived was not bad. Little white houses built around nicely cut greens. Most of the houses looked really neat and attractive: white curtains on the windows, well-kept lawns, flowerbeds. Some houses went one step further: they were clad with ornamental brick fronts instead of the usual white stucco; they had new double-glazed windows and gardens decorated like Japanese gardens or bright with ornamental gnomes or seabirds sculpted from bronze.

His own house was just OK. It was neither ugly nor dirty. But there was nothing pretty about it either. The front garden was covered with tarmacadam, because that was easier to keep than grass. And although there were curtains on the windows, they weren't particularly nice curtains. Inside, it was the same story. Everything was clean and neat, but nothing was special in any way. And there were a few breakages: a gap on the staircase, like missing teeth, where his father had pulled out a couple of banisters once during a fit of rage; a big beige stain on the sofa in the sitting-room, because he had flung a cup of coffee over it recently. The walls were bare of pictures and mirrors; there wasn't a single photograph to be seen anywhere. They never took photos. There wasn't a photograph of Colm or his brother in the house, apart from one or two that had been taken in school.

His mother was watching television.

'What's up?' he said. He knew his father wasn't at home. There was an air of peace in the room which was always absent when he was around.

'Everything's fine,' she said. She was small and thin, his mother. Jet-black hair; a pinched, sallow, face which had been beautiful once upon a time. Her eyes were like black beetles. She was dressed in a tracksuit, as always, and her hair was pulled back into a tight pony-tail.

'Glad to hear it,' he said. 'Here you go.'

He handed her seventy euros. He brought home a hundred and forty today, having worked for more than fourteen hours over the weekend. Seventy to put towards his savings, seventy for her.

'Thanks, love,' she said, putting the notes in her pocket with a jerky movement. She was preoccupied with whatever was on television. Some movie.

'Would you like a cuppa?' he asked.

'That would be lovely, chicken.' She didn't look away from the screen.

He made the tea in the kitchen and brought in two cups on a tray with a plate of biscuits.

There was a commercial break.

'You're a really good lad,' she said with a smile, taking a biscuit.

That sort of compliment embarrassed him, but at the same time it made him happy.

'Did you have a good day?'

'It was fine,' he said. 'Not too busy, but there was enough to keep me going. Ruán came in. Do you remember him? He was in primary with me.'

'Oh, yeah, I know who you mean,' she said. 'From Ashfield Avenue. That's where little Jacob lives.'

'Oh, does he?' Colm hadn't known that. How could he? He was fond of little Jacob, but the two of them were seldom in the house at the same time. He'd often exchange a few words with Jacob's mother, Colette, when she came to pick Jacob up or when she was dropping him off in the morning, but he never paid any heed to where she lived. He should have guessed it was in one of the big private houses and not on this estate.

Some of the mothers on this estate did have jobs: he'd see them in the mornings at the bus stop, dressed to go to work in the factory or the shop or the office or wherever. Somebody must have been minding their children while they were at work. But they wouldn't be able to afford what Jacob's mother paid in child-minding fees, which was two hundred euros a week.

'Yes,' she said. 'Colette and Oliver live next door to Ruán. They were going to some big do there yesterday. Colette showed me the dress she was going to wear.'

Colm thought she was confused. Ruán had told him his folks were away in Turkey. Unless he was lying, or bragging ... But why would he?

He decided to let it drop. It was too complicated and too boring at the same time. He didn't give a fart about these people, really.

It was bedtime. He had to be up at seven in the morning.

'Goodnight, Mam.' He kissed her on the top of the head. 'See you tomorrow.'

He went upstairs to the bathroom. He was still brushing his teeth when the front door opened. He sighed. What a bit of luck that he was already upstairs. He'd pretend to be asleep now, just to be on the safe side.

He put away the toothbrush and sneaked out of the bathroom, sliding along the corridor to the door of his room, which he shared with his brother, Eoin.

He didn't switch on the light.

There was a footstep on the stairs. He jumped into bed still fully dressed, pulled the duvet up under his chin and shut his eyes.

He was really tired. So tired that he fell asleep instantly, even though he was full of anxiety.

He didn't hear his father tramping down the landing into the bathroom. He didn't hear him opening the bedroom door and peering inside.

'The bastards are asleep,' was the first thing he heard, but he pretended to be fast asleep. It was OK; there was no evil in his father's voice. He was still in good humour, although that could change at any moment.

He went back across the landing. The very best thing that could happen now would be that he too would go to bed and fall asleep.

But he didn't do that.

Colm heard his footsteps. On the stairs, going downstairs. Into the sitting-room.

The film was still on. When the sitting-room door opened, he could hear the voices of the actors:

'Rhett, Rhett!'

Gone with the Wind. Not one of Colm's favourites.

'I've always loved you. I never loved anyone else.'

Something like that.

'"I've always loved you! I never loved anyone else!"' said his father in imitation.

His mother didn't say a thing.

By now Colm was wide awake. He was terrified. Now, he knew, there was a good chance that something would happen. He recognised that dangerous edge in his father's voice. The one hope he had now was that whatever happened, it would not be too bad. Damage limitation.

'Rhett, Rhett, will you stay with me? Will you stay here at Tara and look after me?'

Then the sound stopped abruptly. Colm's father had switched off the TV or turned down the volume.

Poor Mam!

She wouldn't complain. The problem was that not complaining was a mistake too. That would annoy him as much as anything else.

'The martyr! So the poor little old lady isn't going to say a word? She ain't like Scarlett O'Hara. This little old lady ain't got no courage!'

That's when his mother spoke.

'Stop!' is what she said.

Crash.

Something smashed. A lamp? A vase? Maybe the television screen.

The sound woke Eoin up.

'What is it?'

'Go back to sleep,' said Colm. 'You're all right.'

But his mother was crying.

'Listen!' Eoin said.

'What have we here? Well, well! Money! Lots of lovely dosh. Where did you get this money?'

Don't tell him.

She didn't.

So he hit her and the scream rose through the house.

'Whore! Where did you get it? You got it from some man, didn't you? What do you get up to when I'm not around? You're a whore, aren't you?'

And he hit her again.

Eoin pulled his duvet up over his head. Colm dashed downstairs and into the sitting-room. He jumped on his father and started beating him. He didn't think of what he was doing, he just battered anything he could reach – the stomach, the arms, the head. His father tried to defend himself but he didn't have a chance. He was big but he was drunk, and Colm was much stronger than he.

'Stop!' his mother started to shout. 'Stop doing that! You'll kill him.'

As soon as Colm heard those words he knew that it was exactly what he wanted. He continued to batter his father. And when he was stretched out on the floor he started to kick him.

His mother ran out of the room.

His father lay on the floor, not moving. Colm stopped beating him.

He switched on the TV. The little girl, Bonnie, was jumping up on her horse. Colm stared at her. He'd never seen such a lovely little girl. Her father was gazing at her, his eyes full of deep love. The love of a father. Not something Colm had ever got.

His father began to stir on the floor. Colm glanced at him. He moved his head from one side to the other but it didn't look as if he was about to wake up.

At that moment two things happened: The horse on the television screen shied and flung

Bonnie to the ground. There she lay. Dead. You knew she was dead because of the accompanying music. At that same moment, a car pulled up and stopped outside the house. Colm pulled back the curtain and looked out.

The Gardaí. Someone had called the Gardaí. A neighbour, maybe, who'd heard the rumpus.

Well, high time, thought Colm. It was a pity nobody had done that sooner. Why hadn't he rung the Gardaí himself? They would be safe now. The Gardaí would take his father and throw him into jail and he wouldn't be able to bother them any more.

The doorbell rang. Colm sighed. His father shifted again on the floor and this time he opened his eyes. Strange. He must have heard the bell too. Colm heard the door being opened, a man's voice saying something, his mother replying in a low tone.

Then two guards were in the sitting-room, his mother standing behind them.

'So, what's going on here?' The Garda looked at Colm. His face had no expression, other than a deep tiredness – that look Gardaí have, as if they know all the answers before they even ask.

'He tried to murder me!' Colm's father spoke vehemently, sitting up. 'He's an animal. We can't keep him under control.'

Colm said nothing. He waited for his mother to speak, to tell the truth.

But she didn't say anything. She just stood there, not a word out of her.

The Garda looked impatiently at Colm.

'That's not true,' said Colm. 'He was attacking my mother.'

Now the Garda looked at his father.

'Were you?'

'That's a complete lie,' he said. 'That fella would say anything. We've been putting up with him for a long time but tonight he's gone and overstepped the mark.'

He tried to stand up but fell back onto the floor. You could smell the beer on him. Didn't the guards smell that?

'I'm seriously injured,' he said. 'Did you call the doctor?' He was addressing his wife.

'I'll ring. If you think you need him,' she said.

'Of course I fucking need him. Are you blind or what?'

He spoke roughly and Colm saw the Gardaí exchanging a glance. For a second he had a ray of hope that they'd see his side of the story.

But his father was cute. He understood that he'd made a mistake.

'Sorry for the French,' he said, in a kind, gentle voice. 'But I'm in agony.'

'OK,' Colm's mother said. 'It's just that it's so late. Where would I get a doctor at this hour?'

'I'll call an ambulance,' said one of the Gardaí.

Colm could see that his father was less than happy with this, for some reason. He was on the verge of saying something but he kept silent. The Garda phoned for an ambulance on his mobile.

'Well.' He looked at Colm's father and mother. 'Do you want us to take him in? Press charges?'

'That's not fair,' said Colm. 'I was trying to protect my mother.'

The Gardaí were still doubtful. The one who was doing the talking turned to Colm's mother.

'Is what he says true?' he asked.

She didn't want to give an answer. Her husband was staring hard at her. Colm was staring at her. It was up to her to tell the truth.

'No,' she whispered in a thin, weary voice.

Colm wasn't arrested.

His father had a big, generous heart, *mar dhea*. He explained, in his most *plamás*y way, that Colm was always a handful, but that he was his son, after all, and that he loved him. He'd give him one more chance.

'Fair enough,' said the Garda.

'But …' Colm started. He was very angry. He wanted them to arrest his father. How could this be happening? Everything was going wrong. Nobody had given him a chance to give his side of the story. These people were Gardaí. Surely they knew something about justice?

'That's enough,' said the talking Garda. He just wanted to get home or back to the station. As far as he was concerned, Colm was just one more delinquent youth. He met them all too often. Or maybe he did suspect that the story was more complicated than it looked, but he was too lazy or too cynical to do anything about it. He didn't want to know. Just one more domestic incident.

The Gardaí left.

Colm's father stood up straight away. He wasn't injured at all. Colm thought he was going to punch him.

But he didn't.

At least one good thing had happened. Colm's father was afraid of him. He knew Colm was dangerous.

'You're a fucking evil bastard,' he said, furious. 'Just you wait and see what happens to you after this, you son of a bitch.'

'What?' Colm stood his ground. He felt brave, oddly enough. He also knew that he was stronger than his father and that was a great feeling.

'You lay a hand on me ever again and you'll rot in jail for half your life,' said his father.

'And you lay a hand on me or on anybody else in this house and you'll rot in your grave for all eternity,' said Colm.

'Fuck you!' His father raised his hand.

But there was a knock on the door.

The ambulance.

Colm laughed.

Down went his father again, on the floor, pretending to be injured. He put his hand over his forehead and suddenly he managed to look half-dead. What a brilliant actor!

A paramedic came in.

'Are you able to walk?' he asked Colm's father.

Colm's father shook his head.

The paramedic left and then returned with another man and a stretcher. They carried him out to the ambulance on that and Colm's mother went with him to the hospital.

The TV was still on and the film was almost over.

'Tomorrow,' Scarlett was saying. 'Tomorrow, tomorrow.'

Tomorrow.

Colm switched off the TV.

What would happen now?

His dad wouldn't come home tonight, was his guess. From what he'd heard about hospitals, he would be still on that trolley, waiting to see a doctor, tomorrow morning. And even though there wasn't a thing the matter with him, he was such a star actor that they'd probably keep him in for a few days, under observation. It all depended on what his father wanted to do, not on the doctors.

So the question was, what was he going to do himself?

He didn't want to stay in this house any longer. He'd tried to protect his mother but she had rejected his protection and his love. When it came to the crunch she'd sided with his father. He didn't want to stick around to take more abuse.

He looked at the time. One o'clock in the morning.

He could go right back to sleep in his own room with Eoin, who had slept through all the *hurlamaboc*. Then he could head off in the morning, try to find a place to live somewhere, although he hadn't a clue how to do that.

Where on earth would he go?

He had money; there was that. Maybe he could stay in a hotel for a while. He'd never stayed in a hotel; he hadn't a clue how you got a room in one. Did you just walk in and say, 'I want a room'?

It'd be easier to doss down in some doorway in the city centre, like a lot of other guys.

Tomorrow.

He'd figure something out tomorrow.

But tonight he just wanted to escape.

That was the only thing he wanted to do.

Get out of there.

7.

HER OWN STORY

EMMA

I have a room of my own. At least there's that. And even though it's tiny, I like it. Correction: I love it. I love the yellow walls and my posters of The Smiths and my bookshelves with all my books. I own more books than anyone in my class. My collection of CDs isn't so big. The thing is, when they buy a CD, I buy a book. Or two. I've got all the classics. You can get them for a couple of euros in the bargain basement of the bookshop on Dawson Street. And then I get a new book too, if I read a good review about it in the newspaper on Saturday.

Not too many people know about my books. Some of my mates would think I was crazy if they knew.

They all know I'm not cool, but even some of the nerds would think I was going a bit far if they knew how I spent my disposable income, i.e. pocket money.

I pretend that I don't get much of same – pocket money. And they believe that, because I don't have a father. They think money comes from fathers. Well, I don't have a father that lives at home. Of course I have one: a father I see once a week. But because he isn't in our house, people think he doesn't exist. Weird. People are weird.

In fact, I have loads of pocket money. I get money from Seán, that's my dad, and Eileen isn't as badly off as people around here think, either. She has a pretty good job in the civil service. She's an AP – that's really high up. All the neighbours think she has some little badly paid job as a secretary or something and she doesn't bother correcting them. I don't either. They're not worth it. Well, a few of them are OK. Jenny, who's a widow and keeps lodgers – I like her. And Mrs O'Brien, who's married to that sleazebag, she's pretty nice too. Sometimes they come around and have a cup of tea or a glass of wine with my mother, and they have a good laugh.

But the others. Ruán and his folks. Such snobs. They have a four-wheel drive, and a huge extension at the back of the house, and houses in Donegal and Budapest and Prague and Istanbul and in lots of other places too, you can bet your boots.

Lísín gets her gear in the Kilkenny shop and Brown Thomas. The best designers. Well, she has nice stuff. Now she goes to House of Fraser in

Dundrum. I know because I've seen her there, trying on an evening dress. I have to admit that I spend a good bit of time there myself. It's not far away and I love all the shops, especially House of Fraser. But I've never actually bought anything there. I browse in House of Fraser and then I buy something in House of Penney.

OK, so Lísín is lucky. I shouldn't give in to the green-eyed monster and I shouldn't let her get to me. But when she didn't invite us to the big party she had the other day, well, that did it for me. That was the last straw. Like, every single person on the road was at that party, except for Eileen.

She was really devastated not to get an invitation.

She pretended not to care, but I could see that she did.

And she knew why she wasn't one of the chosen few – or should I say, the chosen many?

It's not because she's a single mother, even though Lísín isn't quite sure of her ground where single mothers are concerned. But she'd know it's sort of trendy to know one or two of them these days, as long as you don't let it all go too far – like, letting your own daughter be one of them.

No, it's not the single mother thing that puts Eileen in Lísín's bad books.

It's Greg.

Eileen's new 'friend'.

I'm not all that fond of him myself. Correction: I can't stand him. He's a creep. Much younger than

Eileen. They won't tell me his age but my guess is he's about thirty-five, or less. And Eileen is forty-six.

He has black curly hair, slimy, like something disgusting that grows in a rockpool, and a round face. A soft, mush-mush voice. Very sweetie pie. Too sweet to be for real. All that niceness is there for the sake of one thing only: Greg.

My bet is he's trying to get promoted in the office – he's working in the same department as Eileen, which is really fishy. He's an EO and he will be an EO for the rest of his days, unless someone gives him a helping hand, a push up the ladder. That's where Eileen comes in, in Greg's master plan.

And the free lodging comes in handy too, along the way. At the start, he had his own place. Well, that's what I was led to believe. In fact, he was living with his parents. I mean, thirty-five and living with your mammy and daddy – yuck!

'Yeah,' he admitted one day over breakfast. He was hanging around as much as he could from the first day. 'It's pathetic, isn't it?' Well, yes, Greg, it *is* pathetic. 'But you know how much it costs to rent a place these days. I wouldn't get a room for less than a thousand euros a month; it's not worth it.'

But he has a room now, for zero euros a month. A real bargain. And a career promotion thrown in – two for the price of one, if he plays his cards right.

At least we own the house. Correction: at least Eileen owns the house. I'm here on the same basis as Greg. By grace and favour.

But I'm her daughter. And he's her toyboy.

Toyboy. Right.

It's a pity she didn't pick a good-looking toyboy instead of Greg. He's not clever; he's not rich; he's not amusing. And he's not even handsome. In fact, as far as I can see, Greg is a man without a single endearing trait. Yep. And he's the man who's sharing our home with us, right now. He's the man who is always there, when I wake up in the morning and when I'm going to bed at night. The man of the house, you might say.

I have to hide out in my bedroom just to avoid him.

They see it. The neighbours. They see everything. Everyone believes that things have changed, that there's no Valley of the Squinting Windows any more, that the suburbs are strictly private and confidential, everyone out working, minding their own business, not snooping on the neighbours.

But, newsflash! It's not like that at all. Half the women on this road don't have jobs. Lísín doesn't, because she's rolling in it and wouldn't demean herself with actual work. Others say they have a career, but they don't actually go to work most of the time: they're on half-time, or job sharing, or taking a career break. I've noticed that the women on this road often take a year off as soon as the kids start going to school so they'll have a nice little rest for themselves. Then they get an extension to their leave, and then another extension, and before you know it the career girls have morphed into 'full-time home-makers'. The truth is, they'd rather spend their days running off to the hairdresser, or to creative writing classes, or the gym than do an honest day's work. No, there's not much feminism on Ashfield Avenue! Too much money around. Feminism is something that belongs somewhere else, far away from this extremely desirable suburb.

We do have one career girl. Ashfield Avenue's token career girl (apart from my mother who, of course, doesn't count). That's Colette, Jacob's mum and Ruán's next door neighbour. She drops Jacob off to the council estate, Scobieville, during the day. You'd think she'd be worried that he'd pick up something from The Poor over there. She must be getting a real bargain. Most of the mothers who work use child-minders in the private semi-Ds across the main road. That way they keep all the business within the middle classes where it should be, according to them. A kid from the upper middle classes of Ashfield Avenue (where only one kid is not upper middle class: me) goes around to be minded by the lower middle classes around the corner. But poor little Jacob is farmed out to some scobie. I'd love to see him in ten years or so. What sort of an accent will he have? Will those folk that mind him influence the way he thinks about things? Will he spend his free time in the park slugging flagons of cider, shooting up drugs? Will he want to work? That's what's wrong with them, isn't it? They're too lazy to work.

But of course there'll be a solution, as far as Jacob is concerned. Because long before he's ten, Colette will take a career break. Just you wait. She's a television presenter at the moment, star of Ashfield Avenue on weekdays, baker of apple tarts on Saturdays, sailor on Sundays, when they all go out in their nice yacht. But wait till Jacob goes to school – to whatever the latest fasionable school is, needless to say. Colette will take a break then. A little holiday. And Jacob won't have to head off to the knackers to learn how to be lazy; he'll have his mother at home, giving him personal demonstrations.

Ruán. He looks nice. I like his hair, black and heavy. I like the way he has to brush it out of his eyes every few minutes. And he has interesting, big eyes, like a mixture of green and blue, which sort of change from time to time, like Cicero's eyes, at least according to a book I read by Robert Graves – and I guess he'd know. And he's nice and tall and athletic looking, even though I don't think he's into sports, thank God. I'd like to go out with him but I don't think it's going to happen. Lísín wouldn't stand for it. And my own friends think it's a bad idea. According to them, he's a loser. When they spotted me talking to him at the station they gave me a terrible slagging and said he needed a haircut. He's too long and skinny, they say, a beanstalk.

Just jealous, if you ask me.

On the other hand, maybe they see something that I don't. Maybe they're trying to tell me that I'm not in his league. He goes to that private school in Blackrock: big fees, rugby, all that.

Yesterday I met Seán. My dad. We went to a play in town. A tri-lingual play about prisoners in a POW camp in Wales after 1916. English, Irish and Welsh were the languages of the play. I'm good at Irish – I went to a *Gaelscoil* when I was a kid – but of course I don't know a word of Welsh, and neither does Seán. Still I liked the Welsh bits a lot. It sounded beautiful, like a stream babbling along down the mountainside. And actually the guy who was speaking Welsh, the actor, was talking about a river most of the time (there were surtitles, so I did know what they were all saying). He got all the poetic lines, Seán said. Then he topped himself and that was the end of the play. Too romantic, Seán said. The poet who suffers from depression and then kills himself is a romantic stereo-type. Seán knows what he's on about because he's a poet himself. He writes poetry all the time and it gets published and he goes around giving readings and all that. The thing is, he writes in Irish. *As Gaeilge.* If he wrote in English he'd be famous and maybe even rich. But he doesn't; he writes in Irish and so nobody has ever heard of him. People on Ashfield Avenue would never have heard of him – they wouldn't even know he was a writer. Or the people at school. But of course most of the folks around here haven't heard of anyone, they'd hardly know who Seamus Heaney was. Shakespeare, they might have heard of. 'To be or not to be, that is the question.' That's more or less the extent of their literary education, if you ask me.

'I'd like to learn Welsh,' I said to Seán, on the way back to the train.

He said, 'Do it then. You can study it in university. Just do it.'

'Right, I will,' I said.

He's very understanding. But Eileen isn't. Eileen says, do business studies, or law, or medicine if you can get it.

'Then at least you'll have a profession when you're finished,' she says.

I would like to have a profession. Eileen did a BA in French and Spanish and she got first-class honours but she still ended up with a job as an EO in the civil service, and she never really got to use her subjects professionally. She doesn't want that to happen to me.

Seán doesn't care.

He did the same thing but somehow he feels he uses everything because he is a poet. It's all grist to the mill if you write poetry, is what he says. Every single thing to read or learn or experience. It all matters and you have to be open to it all.

The slight problem is: no money. He has a little house in Sallynoggin. He and Eileen split up ages ago – lucky for him because he bought the house just in time, before the house prices went up. If it wasn't for that he'd have nowhere to live. He does a bit of teaching; he goes around giving writing workshops in schools and libraries. Sometimes he gets a good gig as a writer in residence somewhere, but every-thing is temporary. His income is a few thousand euros a year. Plus some sort of a grant he gets from the arts council, but it's not much.

But he's happy.

He's free.

I want to be like him.

I'm never going to get married.

I'm not going to have kids. I'd hate to have a daughter like me.

This is what I'd like: to have a nice boyfriend, as a friend, no strings attached, and to be a famous nov-elist. I'm going to write novels. You get more money for them than for poetry, at least.

'Yeah, you'll make a fortune. Write chick lit,' says Seán.

I'm not going to write chick lit. I'm going to write a novel that will win the Booker Prize. Every year I read the books on the shortlist. I'm already in training.

Greg and Eileen are in the sitting-room, watching *Gone with the Wind.* I quite like that movie but I'm not going to watch it with Greg in the room. I'd rather die.

I'm going to take Ruán up on his invite. I'm going to head down to the great after-the-party party in Lísín's house beautiful.

8.

A KNOCK ON THE DOOR

RUÁN

They were listening to music and the volume was way up. They didn't hear the doorbell. But, as it happened, someone in the hall saw the shadow on the doorstep. He opened the door and let in the person who was standing outside.

It was Colm.

Colm thanked the girl who opened the door. She had long red hair and she smiled warmly at him but girls scared him at the best of times so he just passed her by and went into the sitting-room. Ruán was gobsmacked to see him. For a minute he couldn't even remember having invited Colm but he welcomed him to the party anyway.

'Hi,' he said, giving him a hug. 'Great that you came. There's beer in the kitchen.'

'That's OK,' said Colm. 'I don't drink beer.'

He sat on the floor with his back to the wall, looking around the room. People were sprawled on the blue sofa, the white sofa, the yellow sofa. The floor. Suntanned arms and denim legs blended into one another, girls' hair wrapped around guys' shoulders. You couldn't tell where one body ended and the next began. There were candles lighting and empty beer bottles all over the place. The music pumping, the air sweet with the smell of beer and spicy with the smell of pot.

Colm sighed. It was the kind of mess he hated, but there was something harmonious and easeful about the scene. He felt his limbs relaxing. The angry, frightened, sad thoughts that were racing through his brain like a steeplechase of rats started to blur. Soon they disappeared into the soft light of the candles. And in no time at all after that, Colm finally fell asleep.

When Ruán woke up the next day he was in his own bed in his own room. Neither Emma nor anyone else was with him. The sun was streaming through the window, high in the sky. He glanced at his watch. Ten o'clock.

He could easily have gone right back to sleep but he forced himself out of the bed because he heard the telephone ringing. There wasn't an extension in his room so he ran into his parents' bedroom. There were two guys asleep in the bed and another on the floor. They didn't stir.

'Hello?' There was a frog in his throat.

Nobody replied.

✳

Down in the kitchen, Colm was sitting at the counter drinking a glass of water.

'Grab some food,' said Ruán. 'Coffee or cereal or something. Eat your breakfast.'

'Thanks,' said Colm. 'Can I stay here for a while?'

'Sure,' said Ruán. 'There's lots of people still here. Stick around as long as you like.'

'A week or two?' said Colm.

Ruán hadn't anticipated that.

'Oh! Hmm. Well, my folks will be back at the end of the week. You'd have to head off then,' he said.

'OK,' said Colm. 'That'll probably be long enough.'

There was something about Colm. He was very reserved and you could never tell what he was thinking. He'd changed completely from when he was little. Then, he used to chatter and laugh all the time and his eyes shone like stars in the midnight sky. Now his eyes were dull and never looked at you directly. He, who had been a chatterbox, was shy, a man of few words.

'Why … like, why do you want to stay here?' he asked him.

'I've nowhere else to go,' said Colm. 'At the moment.'

'Right,' said Ruán, impressed. Colm still had a confident way of speaking, for a shy guy. 'Well, you know, like I said, you're welcome to stay here until the old dears come back.'

'I'll do that,' said Colm. 'I'm looking for a flat.' Ruán's mouth fell open. 'Or a room or something.'

'Well, in that case ...'

It occurred to Ruán that he really didn't know Colm well at all. Should he let him stay in the house? Maybe he was dangerous. But dangerous, how? In what way? Ruán hadn't a clue. Maybe he'd steal stuff?

'I had a row with my father,' said Colm, reading Ruán's mind. 'A big row. They don't know I'm here. They don't know where I am.'

This was getting very complicated.

'Well, no worries. I won't tell anyone,' said Ruán.

At that, there was a knock on the hall door.

'Just hold on,' said Ruán. 'Be right back.'

There was a Garda outside.

'The Gardaí!' said Ruán, very loudly so that Colm would hear.

He heard. And he ran out the back door, over the wall and into the next garden, like a shot.

'Are you Ruán Allbright?' one of the guards asked. The talking Garda. He was young looking. The other guard was oldish, and they both looked very nervous.

'I am,' he said.

'Can we come inside?' he asked.

Ruán nodded and the two of them went right into the sitting-room without further ado.

9.

ON THE RUN

COLM

Colm managed to clamber into the garden next door. It was huge, just like Ruán's garden, but the only exit was through a small side door, leading to the front garden. He knew he wouldn't be able to make his way down the garden to that side door without being observed. There was a conservatory at the back of the house and he thought he could see someone moving around in there, behind the big green plants that pressed against the windows. But he couldn't be sure.

He slid around by the hedge that surrounded the lawn, trying to hide in the shelter of the shrubs and trees. And he succeeded. He made it to the side door without being noticed, out through the front garden onto the road.

The Garda car was still parked in front of Ruán's house. Colm knew he could not be seen from the windows of that house, but the Gardaí might emerge at any moment, looking for him. He dithered, wondering if he should make a run for it or try to conceal himself here. He stood behind a huge plant, some sort of tropical grass that grew in the gardens here, along by the coast. He heard a seagull screaming and thought he could hear the waves beating against a distant beach. The seagull floated over Ashfield Avenue, sure and confident as an aeroplane, and sailed smoothly through the sky on its way to the sea.

Colm decided to risk it. He started to run. There was nobody on the road. Everyone was at work or at school. He himself was due at the SPAR at half past four – he had most of the day to find a place to live.

He reached the train station, glancing over his shoulder nervously all the time. The Gardaí were nowhere to be seen. They must be busy searching Ruán's house or something, looking for him.

But on other other hand, how would the Gardaí even suspect that he was in Ruán's house? How did they find that out?

He didn't know. Someone must have seen him going in there last night. Jacob's mother, maybe. She lived next door. Or perhaps it was just that the neighbours had told them there was a big party in Ruán's last night and that he might have been at it, even though people from his estate seldom mixed with the kids on Ruán's road.

Oh well. Here was the train, on its way into town.

He would have liked to phone his mother to let her know that he was OK but wouldn't be coming home any time soon. That's all there was to say. He was over eighteen years of age; he was fully entitled to live anywhere he liked.

He put his hand in his pocket but his mobile wasn't there.

Fuck.

He'd left it at home on the table beside his bed.

He stared out the window, at the white houses, each with its little kitchen extension butting out into the garden. Gardens full of flowers and shrubs, with patios and furniture, others just a worn down lawn with a swing and a little plastic goalpost at one end. A woman hanging out white clothes on a line. Then the coast – the long golden beach, dog-walkers. Some morning swimmers. An old-looking woman walking out of the sea, taking off her rubber bathing cap and shaking her hair, as if she were a dog. The red and pink wild flowers tumbling down the sides of the hill; the small green speck, smooth as jelly, that was Dalkey Island. He'd never been on the island, though when he was little his mother had always promised they'd go out some Sunday in summer and have a picnic there, him and Eoin and her. He'd longed for that for years, but for some reason they never got around to it. And when he was eleven or twelve he'd stopped hoping.

Dun Laoghaire.

He decided to get out here, although he didn't know why. Maybe he'd be as well off looking for a room around here. He'd be nearer the shop, if he went on working there, although he wasn't sure that he could. It might be better to find a job somewhere far from home.

He had his wallet with all his money in it. More than two thousand euros: he'd always kept his money in cash, hidden in a secret place under a floorboard in his bedroom, just in case. Just in case of an emergency like this one. He'd enough money to live on for several weeks.

He went to a public phone box in the shopping centre near the station and called home.

His mother answered.

'Where are you?' she said, without even saying hello.

'I'm in town,' he said, looking out. He could see the harbour and the big white ship, the Holyhead ferry, waiting by the quay.

'Come home,' she said. 'Please.'

She sounded desperate.

'I'm not coming home, Mam,' he said. 'I'm sorry. It's not my fault. But I can't live in the same house as my father any more.'

It was surprisingly easy to say this, because it was the absolute truth.

She said nothing.

'I'm sorry,' he said again. 'I'm going to find a place to live somewhere in the city, and I'll find a job. I'll be fine.'

'Your dad is still in hospital,' she said slowly.

Colm felt sick and weak.

'Why?'

'He's in danger,' she said flatly.

'How? What is it?'

There was another pause. He couldn't say anything.

'He had a heart attack last night, in the ambulance,' his mother said.

There was a change in her tone of voice as she said this. The edge, the desperation, had disappeared. She sounded like an automaton, a voice on a telephone answering machine. He wondered if someone was listening to her. A Garda?

'Please just come home,' she said. Her voice changed again. 'It's not your fault. Please. Good lad.' She was crying. 'I need you here.'

'All right,' said Colm. 'I'll come home right now.'

He hung up and left the phone booth.

The sun was still shining; people were still walking on the footpaths, and the buses and cars were moving along the road. A green train made its way along the track by the seafront. But his life had changed completely. He was a different person from the one who had walked into that shopping centre five minutes previously. Now he was a criminal. A boy who had killed his father. If his father were to die, he'd be a murderer.

No matter what his mother said. And he had a feeling that she was telling lies. Something in her tone of voice hinted at that – someone was pressurising her to get him to come home. They'd be waiting for him; they'd throw him into jail. Nobody would believe his version of the fight with his father. His own mother hadn't supported him when the Gardaí came last night, so why would she do that today? She pretended to love him but she wasn't a real friend. She was against him. She was loyal to her husband and she was capable of betraying her son at any time, just like she did last night.

Colm walked along mechanically, not thinking about where he was heading. But his feet carried him in the direction of the sea. In front of him lay the harbour, with its hundreds of little boats dancing on the water like girls at a *feis*, the sun making sparkling swordpoints on the sea. It was a merry sight. The world and everyone in it went right on, laughing and living, not giving a hoot about the terror that was weighing down his heart.

The big ferry boat was waiting by the marina; the cars and passengers were lining up, about to go aboard and across the sea to Wales.

His mind wasn't working, but his feet carried him along, to the ticket office in the ferry terminal.

'There's a special offer on one-day tickets,' the woman said. She looked at him curiously. It was clear that she thought he was a bit young to be heading off on the boat for the day, on a schoolday, all alone.

'I'm going for a week,' he said. 'I'm going to visit my mother. She lives over there.' The woman looked sympathetic. 'She's divorced from my dad,' he added.

'OK,' she said and handed him a return ticket. He didn't really need a return, because he didn't know when he'd be returning, or if. But he was afraid to say that. Sixty euros gone already.

It was worth it.

In no time at all he was aboard. He was leaving Ireland.

10.

THE SHELTER OF NEIGHBOURS

EMMA

Half past seven. Yuck. I didn't get home till three o'clock this morning. I'm still knackered. I'm sick with tiredness.

Eileen comes into my room.

'Time!' she says, as she says every morning.

'Uh huh,' I say. 'OK.'

She heads off to the bathroom. I hear footsteps on the stairs, the radio being switched on. Greg, making coffee for himself. He only drinks real coffee and he prepares it in a little machine he's got for himself. Eileen is a tea drinker and I only take green tea or herbal.

But I like the smell of Greg's coffee. It's a nice, peaceful smell. I close my eyes and fall back to sleep instantly.

'Emma! You'll be late for school!' Eileen is dressed in the black suit she wears for the office.

'I don't feel well,' I say. 'I'm sick.'

'Oh, Emma! When did you come home last night?'

'Don't remember. I can't get up,' I say. 'I'm wrecked. I'll study at home.'

She sighs, says no more and leaves the room.

That's the best way to make me feel bad. I feel guilty and lazy, like a loser. Terrrible. But I don't get out of bed.

Ten minutes later I hear the front door closing. A lovely silence falls over the house and I go back to sleep.

Heaven!

Dream. Big boat. A cosy cabin, small but with nice furniture. Somebody is sharing this cabin with me but that person isn't there and I'm worried – I don't know who it is I am sharing with. I know the person should be with me right now, and I feel I am in some sort of danger without them. That's what I feel. So I leave the cabin and go up on deck.

But it's not a deck; it's an examination hall. The room is full of schoolkids, writing away. There is a desk there for me. I know where it is and I sit down at it. But I don't have a pen and I don't even have my examination number. I know what subject we are being examined in. History. But I haven't prepared anything for the exam. I had planned to learn an essay off by heart but now I can't even remember what the topic of that essay was.

Ruán is up at the top of the hall. He's not writing either. He's looking around in confusion, it seems to me.

Through the window I see the ship on which I was a passenger a few minutes ago. But the ship is far away now, it's on the horizon, a huge big ship splitting the sea behind it with its churning white wake. It's disappearing from view, over the edge of the sea and the sky.

I am scared to death.

I wake up, in bad humour. Half past ten. The terror vanishes in a flash, the way it does after a nightmare, but I'm uneasy. Better do a bit of work. The Leaving will start all too soon and I'm far from ready. Even though I do know my history project off by heart. And I remember what it's about! Hannah Sheehy Skeffington: her life.

I make a cup of green tea and put a couple of slices of bread in the toaster. The cat's outside screaming her head off. I let her in and rub some suncream on her ears – she's a white cat and they can get skin cancer easily, from the sun, but Eileen is always rushing in the morning and she forgets to put the stuff on the cat. Fake tan is the best stuff – I use it myself sometimes; the cat and I share a tube.

I really should get down to it now, after my tea. I'm no longer tired and I feel fine but I'm in no mood to study. Well, nothing new there. I never feel like studying even though I do feel like getting great results and my first choice of courses. But I have to coax myself to work. Do one hour, then take a break and go for a little walk, I tell myself. Or do half an hour and then phone a friend. Usually this works. And after an hour I take a break, or I don't, if I just feel like continuing with the work. You get into the habit. The hard part is getting started.

I have a table and chair in my own room, beside the window. Sitting down at the table is the first hurdle. I sit down and of course look out the window, and I see a Garda car parked outside Ruán's house and two guards walking down his driveway.

Hmm. What's going on? Somebody must have snitched about the party. Who'd do that? Colette, with that horrible baby of hers. Poor little dear couldn't get his beauty sleep. There wasn't even any real noise because it wasn't a real party.

I decide to phone Ruán.

'Hi, Emma,'

He won't let me speak.

'Are you at home?'

I tell him I am.

'Would you come around?'

I know the answer to that. No, I've got work to do. But I say, 'Sure. I'll be around in a few minutes.'

But first I brush my hair and put on just a tiny bit of make up.

Ruán's parents are dead.

Lísín and Pól.

They were killed in some sort of accident in Istanbul, sometime yesterday. They were in a taxi on the way to the airport and there was a bomb. Lots of people were killed – I remembered hearing something about it on the news – but they didn't identify Lísín and Pól until the early hours of the morning. And Ruán got the news around ten o'clock.

He tells me all this sitting in the front room. He's very pale but he seems to be all right; he seems to be able to cope with it all but I can't imagine how.

He can either go out to Turkey or not. The guards said it was up to him.

Suddenly I remember his little brother.

'What about Cú?'

Cú knows. He's staying on with his friend for the moment and Ruán is going to see him this afternoon.

'Wouldn't you want to go over there? To see … the bodies. Don't you have to identify them?'

He shook his head.

'I don't want to fly to Turkey,' he said. 'They don't need me to identify them. Somebody has already done that, a colleague of my father's who lives out there. And somebody in the embassy will make the arrangements for getting them home.'

I can't think of anything to say.

He goes on, 'I'm on my own!' He laughs uneasily.

He hasn't got any aunts or uncles. Just one grand-mother, Lísín's mother. He loves her but she's not on top of things any more even though she lives in-dependently. She doesn't understand things very well, he says; she wouldn't have a clue how to deal with this.

I don't know this woman so I don't know whether he's right about her or not. He hasn't even spoken to her yet. He's not even sure if she knows that Lísín is dead.

'Shouldn't you talk to her?' I say.

'I couldn't,' he says.

All he wants to do is sit in the house and stare out at the sky. That's what he's doing anyway. I take his hand in mine and he doesn't pull it away.

I look out the window too.

The sun has disappeared. Huge clouds crowd the sky, so thick that all you can see is white and grey and silver. The sea is dark and gloomy, and far, far away on the edge of the sky is the ferry, making its way over to Wales, as it does three or four times a day.

We sit there, silently, for a very long time. For an hour almost. Ruán is thinking about what has hap-pened, or about what is going to happen next. I don't really know because he doesn't talk. What I am thinking about is the future. His future. Him and Cú here in the house. Will they be able to stay on here? Cú is too young, but maybe Ruán is mature enough to be his guardian. Old enough? There's a lot I don't know about these things.

Such as what would happen to me if Eileen died? I can't imagine it. I get panicky just thinking of the possibility.

'Will I make tea or coffee or something?' I ask.

Such a banal question that it disgusts me. So that's what you do when a terrible tragedy happens to your friend. You offer them a cup of tea.

'All right,' says Ruán.

I stay with him for the remainder of the day. When I call Eileen to let her know what's happening she's very understanding.

'Just stay with him for as long as he needs you,' she says.

Does she mean overnight too? I'm not sure.

The house is a mess after the events of last night, so I try to tidy it up a bit. Such a neat, lovely house – it's really strange to see it in such disarray. Ruán finds it upsetting that it's in such a state. Lísín isn't going to come home to give out to him about it ever again, but now he wants the house to be just the way she likes it. The way it usually is.

He gives me a hand with the cleaning. That seems weird. His parents have just been killed and he starts doing housework. But maybe it helps. He hoovers while I do the rest. It doesn't take that long to restore it to some sort of order, although there's a lot more to do before it's back to its original spick and span self.

We are there all afternoon. Ruán becomes mechanical. I can see that the truth hasn't sunk in for him yet. He doesn't cry; he doesn't even talk about his parents. Instead he natters on about the house-cleaning and about school. He seems to have forgotten Cú and that he was supposed to visit him. He's not sad but he's terrified, I think. And confused. Everything is very confusing. The guards said someone would come to see him – he doesn't remember who; a social worker? – but nobody comes.

Things feel chaotic and horribly calm, deadly calm, at the same time. It's as if the whole world is waiting for something to happen, even though this thing has already happened. It's as if Ruán is waiting for Lísín to come back and organise everything, tell him what to do, restore things to normality. But Lísín won't be coming back. Nobody will.

The house seems enormous, and being there today feels like being in outer space. There's too much room in it, and too much time, and too much … ambivalence. Uncertainty. We're both drowning in air that feels light and dizzying, or that feels like a vacuum. Maybe this is what infinity feels like.

Not nice.

I stay with Ruán and I know I'm no real help; I'm lost, just like him. Lost and waiting to be rescued.

And, finally, someone comes. Eileen. My mother. Of course. It's inevitable that she would be the one to come and save us.

I'm so grateful to her; I'm so glad I still have a mother. Someone who knows what has to be done. She just gives Ruán a big, long hug, although she hardly even knows him. And then she takes command.

First she telephones the grandmother, Lísín's mother. And she hadn't even heard about the accident. She'd heard something on the news but not the names. And anyway, she is deaf so she doesn't hear things properly and that's why she doesn't know what's going on half the time. She hadn't understood that Lísín and Pól were in Turkey, even. She thought Lísín had said they were going to spend a week in Thurles.

'Did something happen in Thurles?' she asked. 'I didn't hear anything about that. And I had the radio on all day. Why didn't somebody phone me?'

Maybe somebody had been trying to phone and she didn't hear what they were saying, Eileen said. Or maybe she didn't hear the phone or the doorbell.

Eileen speaks in a good, loud voice so that Ruán's granny can hear. She tells her Ruán and Cú will go to see her later. Then she and Ruán and I go to see Cú.

He seems embarrassed by the whole thing. He doesn't want to talk about it. He keeps asking about a summer football camp he's supposed to be going to. Will he still be able to go?

'Yes.' Ruán is very definite about this. 'Of course you'll be going to the football camp. You have to get in as much training as you can for your career as a professional footballer.'

This cheers Cú up. It gives him courage. It's as if he's got a new father already. Ruán.

Ruán's grandmother calls him on the mobile phone. She wonders where he is and when he's coming to see her. Ruán doesn't feel like making another visit but Eileen says it's better to call around. So we all go to Ruán's granny.

Their granny lives in an old suburb close to the city centre. She has a funny house – it looks as if nothing in it has changed since about 1960. Carpets with swirly patterns, orange and black, all over the house, even in the bathroom. A three-piece suite. Wallpaper with stripes or flowers or big green leaves, and every surface packed with ornaments, china dolls and dogs and cats, a teapot shaped like a thatched house, silver bowls and candlesticks. Her house is like an antique shop, or a junk shop. Except that it is as neat as a pin. Lísín didn't fall far from the tree.

I know the minute I step inside the dark hall that the lads won't want to live in this house.

But their grandmother is lonely and sad and very puzzled.

She does what you do when there's a tragedy: she gives us tea and biscuits. And she repeats, over and over again, 'What's the world coming to? Nobody's safe. It could happen anywhere. It could happen to any of us.'

But she wants Cú and Ruán to stay with her.

'You'll be better off here,' she says. 'What would you be doing, going back to that big, empty house?'

She has a point, I have to admit. She doesn't give them a chance to express their own wishes. She doesn't seem to listen to anyone. Maybe that's because she can't hear what they're saying.

'I've plenty of rooms to spare and I can get food in easily; I'm so close to the shops here. It's not like Rathbeg. There's a good shop up on the corner and the shopping centre is just a stone's throw away. Ruán could easily run down and do the messages, couldn't he?'

'Well, I'd like to –' he starts, but he doesn't get a chance to finish the sentence.

'I've the beds made up for you already and I've got in stuff for dinner this evening. Are you hungry, boys? I've got chips and burgers; I know you like chips and burgers. They're nice burgers, they're not frozen, they're nice and fresh, and I've got ice-cream as well, I know you like a bit of ice cream after your dinner.'

Eventually Eileen steps in.

'Ruán wants to go home to his own house,' she says.

And Ruán and Cú nod. Their own house is what they want. It's big and cold and empty but it's what they're used to. Eileen speaks loudly and clearly. Their granny doesn't hear.

'What's that? What did you say?'

Eileen repeats it, kindly.

'They'll call tomorrow morning. I will phone too.'

She feels sorry for the grandmother but she feels sorry for Ruán and Cú as well. There are two sorrows fighting with each other.

'This is my number.' She writes it down on a piece of paper and hands it to their grandmother. 'You phone any time you want to.'

Then we say goodbye to her and drive home to Ashfield Avenue. I look behind as we drive down her road. She is standing at her gate, all alone, and I think I see tears running down her cheeks.

11.

THE WAVES

COLM

Colm stayed out on deck for most of the crossing. He watched Dun Laoghaire slipping away from him, becoming more mysterious and magical as it disappeared. He'd never known there were so many steeples in Dun Laoghaire, rising like prayers against the backdrop of the mountains and sky, floating layers of purple and green, grey and white. He saw the shape of the town as if it were drawn with a soft brush, an outline which was invisible while you were in it. Even though he was full of anxiety, the beauty of the scene lifted his heart.

And his spirits lifted even further when he couldn't see it any more.

Less than an hour and the coastline of Ireland had vanished. *Ban Chnoic Éireann Ó!* Farewell, Ireland! Who would have thought it was so easy to get out of the place! And how odd it was that he had never made this voyage before, nor had his mam. They acted as if they were imprisoned in Ireland. When all you had to do was walk into the ferry terminal, buy a ticket and off you go! It was like catching the bus.

People like Ruán, and even Emma, were constantly on the move. Always going abroad. But Colm's folks didn't have that habit. It wasn't just the shortage of money that prevented his mother from travelling abroad, or anywhere else. It was something else. And what was that?

He didn't know. But at least he was breaking away now, even if it wasn't for the best of reasons.

He wished he was just going away on a holiday, on his first trip abroad, instead of escaping from the law.

It wasn't long till the coast of Wales came into view. He was disappointed to see that it looked very like the coast that he had just left behind – true, it had a more remote, sort of a country look to it, but it was like the countryside at home. Wicklow or somewhere like that. It didn't seem the least bit foreign. Boggerland.

The ferry stopped, the ship's door was opened and the foot passengers walked across the gangplank and into the Welsh terminal. He stayed with the line of people – most of the passengers on the boat had cars and were down in the bowels of the ship, on the car deck, waiting to drive off. He followed the walkers down to a foyer. Above him he could see a town on a hill – Holyhead. But everyone was continuing on to the railway station. A train was waiting there and people were boarding it already.

'Where is this train going?' he asked a woman.

'London.' She pointed at the information display.

London. The name, in its ordinary black letters, looked magical. It was as if he had stepped into the pages of a fairytale, or into a film.

He must have looked taken aback because she asked him if he had a ticket to London.

'No,' he said.

'You can buy one back there.' She pointed to a ticket office. 'It's a pity you didn't buy it in Dun Laoghaire: it would have been cheaper there.'

Colm thanked her and went quickly to the ticket office. He found out that a ticket to London cost more than a return fare from Dun Laoghaire to Holyhead.

But why would he go to London?

He decided to stick around for a while before making any further plans. The ticket seller told him there was a train every hour, although only a few of them were express to London. He could come back later, if he felt like it, and get a ticket then.

He crossed a bridge from the station to the town and walked around the streets. Caer Gybi, it was called, as well as Holyhead. It wasn't much of a town, in his estimation. Some little shops, supermarkets, an off-licence. A few pubs and cafés. Plenty of houses were B&Bs and they displayed their rates: £25, £30. He didn't have any sterling, just euros. He hadn't thought of that, or remembered that they didn't use euros over here in the UK. He should look for a bank. But it was after three o'clock already. The banks would be closed.

He didn't really like this town. It was small and exposed. Worn out and shabby. Very different from Dun Laoghaire. He didn't feel happy here.

The happiness he had felt on the boat deserted him as he walked back over the gusty bridge towards the terminal and the station. A wave of homesickness overcame him. He thought of the Spar and of Molly, the woman who was so kind to him. He thought of his mother. And school. There'd be no Leaving Cert for him now. It was too weird! He'd spent the past six years studying and listening to teachers begging him to do his best, impressing upon him that his whole future depended on the results of these examinations. And now he wouldn't even be doing them!

How could you be homesick for exams? But he was.

The light in this place, a cold white light, filled him with foreboding. No, he could not stay here.

Halfway across the bridge was a little piece of sculpture with a stone seat. 'Peace to all who pass here' was engraved on it in English and in a language he guessed to be Welsh. He sat there for a minute, in the wind, listening to the seagulls screaming. They sounded sad too, and homesick, for some far-off place they had lost and would never see again. A big, fat seagull perched on the wall of the bridge close to him and looked at him. It looked suspicious and cross, as if someone had been annoying it. Most seagulls look like that.

London. London would be more like Dublin than this sad place. He'd feel more at home there. So he thought, sitting on the bridge, even though he was very seldom in Dublin. The fact was, he'd spent most of his life right where he had been born, in the suburb of Rathbeg. He'd never spent more than an afternoon or an evening anywhere else.

He went back to the terminal and changed three hundred euro at a Bureau de Change. Somehow he didn't want to change all his money to sterling yet. And he thought it would be safer not to. The guy might wonder where someone like Colm had got his hands on a few thousand smackers.

He looked at the timetable on the wall of the station.

Trains actually went to many places other than London. Manchester. Chester. Shrewsbury. They all stopped at lots of stations en route. And every train stopped at a place called Bangor, which looked as if it wasn't too far from this town.

Bangor.

There was a nice ring to the name.

He observed that the trip to Bangor took about half an hour.

He went back to the ticket office.

'Oh, you again!' the man said, recognising him. Colm wished he hadn't. If the guards were after him they might find it easy to track him down. At the moment, for instance, he was the only person in the station – everyone from the ferry had gone on the London train. He was easy to spot – a young man without any luggage, not even a backpack.

'I'd like a return ticket to Bangor,' he said, letting on that he planned to return.

'Twelve pounds,' said the man.

Jesus, it cost to travel on these trains.

He handed over the cash and got the ticket. Within half an hour he was on the train, moving quickly through fields and slopes, past little stations with funny names, towards Bangor.

The train came to the sea again, or to a wide, wide river. He'd have to look at a map sometime to see what it was. They crossed a huge steel bridge and the next thing the driver was saying, in his English accent, 'Bangor. Stopping at Bangor.'

The moment Colm stepped off the train he knew he had made the right decision.

The train station was nice. There were red geraniums in pots on the platform and a decent-looking shop where you could get newspapers and sweets and stuff. There was a bus stop outside on the road and a few taxis lined up. He could see a sign for a hotel. The town stretched out to the right of the station and there were suburban houses nestling in trees on a hill to his left.

It was evening but the sun was shining again.

He walked down to the right, in the direction of the town. There was one long, busy street, full of shops and pubs. A few small hotels, but he didn't want to stay in a hotel. Where would he spend the night? The weather was so mild that he could sleep rough, but he didn't fancy that. On the other hand, he'd waste money fast if he slept in a B&B or a hotel.

He came to an old stone church about halfway along the main street. Bangor Cathedral, a plaque told him. It was small for a cathedral, it seemed to Colm. Much smaller than Christchurch, one of the only cathedrals he'd seen. It reminded him of old ruins in Glendalough, except it wasn't a ruin but a perfect church, surrounded by grass and trees. In the distance, on the steep slope behind it, he saw a big, dark-red building that looked like a castle. A castle. Since he was still feeling that he was in a fairy story he thought he might as well walk up and see what was up there. He began to make his way up the hill.

The street he found himself on appealed to him more than the main street. It was quiet and had a more casual feel to it. Health food shops, boutiques with somewhat unusual clothes. Galleries, a music shop.

And on this street he found the place he was looking for. Not a castle: a hostel. A lovely little hostel, with geraniums outside – Colm loved geraniums – and red wooden windows with gingham curtains on them.

There was a vacancy – twenty pounds for the night, breakfast not included. He took it straight away.

The room was small and cramped enough, but it was clean, with white walls and red curtains. And it was his room, for tonight. He had a comfortable bed; he had a place to stay.

Out he went. He could smell the sea from here and after a while he reached a pier and the inlet he'd crossed earlier, full of sailing boats, like Dun Laoghaire harbour. He bought fish and chips from a chipper near the shore, sat down and ate them. He realised he hadn't eaten since yesterday evening, when he'd had a sandwich in the tearoom at the back of the Spar.

The Spar.

He filled up with tears, thinking of the shop. The shelves waiting to be stacked with bread. The counter he stood behind, talking to friendly people. That was where he'd been happy, in the Spar.

He felt completely exhausted. Very slowly, he made his way back to the hostel and collapsed into bed.

He slept for twelve hours.

To his shock, it was nine o'clock when he woke up – Colm was always an early riser and was seldom in bed later than seven.

Downstairs he went and bought breakfast. Then he made his bed and booked the room for another night.

He went out into the town. The first thing to do was to get some sort of job.

He went back to the main street, where most of the shops and businesses were. Cafés, pubs, small supermarkets, clothes shops. There were a few department stores in a shopping centre. He looked out for notices – Staff Wanted. He was used to seeing that sign in windows all over Dublin but it wasn't so common in Bangor. In fact, he only saw the sign once, in a tandoori restaurant, but the place was shut. He remembered the details and continued on.

He began to go into shops and ask if they needed staff.

No.

A few of them asked for his name and phone number.

He gave his name and invented a mobile phone number. He knew it looked strange not to have a telephone number of any description. It would be a good idea to buy a new phone – but that would cost money, and he'd have to give his name and address in order to register. At least he remembered doing that at home. Then he'd be traceable.

It wasn't easy to hide and remain anonymous, even when you were abroad.

He spent the morning searching fruitlessly for work. At lunchtime he bought a few bread rolls and a can of Coke and took his lunch on a park bench beside the cathedral. Then he bought a newspaper, hoping there might be some ads for jobs in it.

In the newspaper there was an article about a big accident in Turkey, in which twenty people had been killed, including some British and and a few Irish holiday-makers.

This had happened on Sunday. He remembered hearing about it then, just after it happened. Ruán's folks were in Turkey on Sunday. But so were thousands of Irish people. It was a very popular holiday destination.

Then he found a column in the paper with a few job advertisements. There were some relating to Bangor. 'Shop assistant wanted. Experience necessary. Mini-market, college area.'

'Still room waiter. No experience necessary. Central Hotel.'

There were phone numbers to ring. He circled the ads, found a call box and made the phone calls. Both advertisers asked him to call in person that very afternoon. They wanted staff immediately.

He went back to his room in the hostel. He hadn't changed his clothes in three days, nor shaved. He had showered this morning because the hostel provided soap and a towel. Now he purchased a razor, but decided to wait till he had a job before investing in new clothes. When he'd shaved he thought he looked reasonably presentable – his clothes didn't actually stink, as far as he could tell, and they were neat, since he was still in his working gear. He looked at himself in the mirror – his fair hair was very short because he went to the barber's every month; his face was a bit pale from being indoors so much, but in his blue shirt and navy jacket he looked neat and presentable enough. He told himself nobody would guess that he was a boy who had killed his father, was on the run from the police and hadn't had a change of clothes in three days.

He went to the shop first, since that sounded like the better job.

It was a small supermarket, as the ad had indicated. There were boxes outside on the pavement – vegetables, fruit, flowers. Inside, the place was dim as a cave and crammed with groceries. You could hardly find a way around the stacks.

The checkout was just inside the entrance door, and a man with dark hair and skin was sitting at it.

Colm introduced himself.

'I spoke to someone on the phone about an hour ago, about the job that's advertised,' he said. 'I came to do an interview.'

The man scrutinised him.

'Are you in trouble with the cops?' was the first thing he said.

Colm was startled. He wondered if his picture had been in the papers already. Or on television.

'No,' he said. 'I'm a student and I'm looking for a summer job.'

'Where do you come from?' the man asked, without batting an eyelid.

'Dublin,' said Colm. And added, 'In Ireland,' in case the man didn't know where it was.

The man wasn't too pleased with this information, apparently, because he looked annoyed. But at that moment a customer came into the shop – a woman in search of cocoa.

'We have cocoa,' said the man. He looked at Colm. 'Could you fetch a tin of cocoa for this lady? It's at the back of the shop beside the tea and sugar.'

A test.

Colm went looking for a tin of cocoa, which was easier said than done. There were only three tins in stock, and they were hidden behind packets of tea. But he found them and brought one back to the woman.

She said something in a foreign language. Then she spoke English.

'You're not Welsh?' she said. 'You look Welsh.'

The man behind the checkout could speak Welsh, even though he didn't look at all Welsh.

'Thank you, anyway, even if you're not Welsh,' said the woman, with a big smile, and left the shop.

'All right,' said the man, in the same tough guy tone he had used all the time. 'If you want it, the job is yours. Seven pounds an hour, forty hours a week on various shifts, to be decided. You need to be flexible for this job. We open at eight in the morning, close at midnight. Are you happy with that?'

Colm did the sums in his head. Seven pounds an hour was good pay, given that it was sterling.

'I'm happy,' he said.

'When can you start?' The man looked at Colm, up and down, as if sizing up his strength. 'Can you start tomorrow?' he asked, without waiting for an answer.

'Sure,' said Colm. 'The sooner the better.'

'That's what I like to hear,' said the man. He had an accent Colm had never heard before, but it was very easy to understand and he liked it. It was musical. They shook hands.

'Of course I will have to get some information from you,' said the man. 'Do you have a social security number?'

'I'm Irish. I don't have a number over here,' said Colm.

'Just came over on the boat?' The man nodded.

'Yeah.'

'Never mind. I have the forms. Take them and fill them in and give them to me tomorrow. Tomorrow you work from eight till five. There is a half hour break for lunch, of course.'

'Fine,' said Colm, although it sounded like a very long day. 'I'll see you tomorrow then.'

12.

THE GAP

EMMA

We left Ruán and Cú in their own house and Eileen and I came home. I felt bad about abandoning them there in the big house. It felt terribly lonely. Lísín was such a big personality. Without her, you feel there's a huge hole, a gap, in the house.

That's what I felt.

I don't know if Ruán or Cú noticed the same thing. I don't think so. Actually I think they don't feel anything at the moment; they're sort of paralysed. They haven't been able to take it all in.

I wonder if they should have stayed with their grandma, after all. I don't like to think of her on her own either, after losing her only daughter. Maybe we should have brought her out here, to be with them in the house? It doesn't feel right to me, leaving her on her own like that. She's about eighty.

Journalists have been trying to interview Ruán and Cú but Eileen has forbidden them to talk to them, and she has advised Ruán not to let anyone into the house.

A few other Irish people were killed in the bomb episode, apparently. It was a big news story. Interviews with people in Turkey, with relatives of the dead. Images – the burnt-out taxi, a building beside it that exploded, devastation, the sun dancing on broken windows, bodies in black bags, an officer saying there would be an investigation although a bomb was not suspected – even though everyone says it was a bomb. The taxi driver was dead. Was he the one responsible?

'Will there be a funeral, and all that sort of thing?' I asked Eileen.

'There will be, after a while,' she said.

'How? Who'll organise all that?' I knew Ruán wouldn't be able to do it. I knew it would be much easier for him if there were nothing formal, no funeral.

'It'll be easy enough,' she said. 'Don't worry. A few phone calls is all it will take. I'll look after it if nobody else will. Haven't they any relatives at all, apart from their grandmother?'

'No,' I said. 'That's what they told me, anyway.'

'Isn't that kind of odd?'

I went to school the next day, even though I wasn't in the mood for it. Ruán stayed at home, naturally. Nobody had discussed the Leaving. Would he do it or not?

I found it hard to concentrate. I always find it hard but today I felt the exams were completely irrelevant and without importance, and I felt the same about school itself, in the context of what had happened to Ruán. Nobody in school knew I was connected to anyone affected by the tragedy in Turkey – nobody was talking about that at all. It was just one of those things you see on the news, a tragedy that happened in a far off place, that you forget about as soon as the news is over. I didn't feel like talking about it to my friends, explaining everything, and so I said nothing.

As soon as I got home I called in to Ruán.

But there was nobody at home.

I was disappointed. I really wanted to talk to him, to be with him. Where were they? Well, they could be anywhere. All kinds of people would be in touch with them. The guards and people from foreign affairs. Lawyers. Priests.

Maybe they'd gone back to their grandmother's.

I rang him on his mobile but he didn't answer.

13.

THE NEXT KNOCK

RUÁN

The funeral was over.

It wasn't as bad as I'd feared but it was bad enough. At least they didn't make me and Cú do anything at it. We were just allowed to sit there, looking sad, shaking hands with people. I was afraid we'd have to do the prayers of the faithful and give eulogies and carry little objects symbolising Pól and Lísín's interests to the altar for the offertory. (What would I have picked? Lísín's Hermès handbag? That was a thing she really loved. The keys of her four-by-four? OK, OK, a snap of all us – I know she loved us more than anything. In front of the new extension, of course. She loved that too. Her perfume. Which I loved. I go into her room every day still to get that scent, the smell of my mother.) But they actually didn't bother with that little ritual and other people took care of all the rest, the speeches and the prayers and so on. Cú and I just sat there beside our nana and before we knew it our folks were buried.

And the next part of our life was beginning. The on-your-own bit. Grown-up-hood.

That's what I thought.

I made one decision fast. My first independent decision. That was not to do the Leaving this year. I was in no humour for it, and they all understood – the teachers, the head. Mícheál acted as a go-between – he was great for someone who normally slagged the life out of me. They knew I wouldn't want to go back to school for the moment. I didn't even have to phone them. But I had mentioned it to the principal at the funeral, outside the church. We were standing right beside the hearse, I remember, where the two coffins were lying side by side, covered with enormous bouquets of white and red roses.

'You're quite right, dear,' the head said gently. But there was a shadow on her face and I knew what she was thinking: 'Another whole year!' But all she said was, 'You're young, there's no rush at all.'

I heard something then. A soft noise from the hearse.

The back door of the hearse was open still. A sudden puff of wind riffled through the flowers, and the roses were whispering.

Or … this is crazy … was it Lísín, protesting? She wouldn't like my decision not to do the Leaving. She wouldn't like it one little bit. Well, I said to myself, as the undertaker closed the door of the hearse, it's an ill wind that blows no good. Lísín has no power over me now, and may God have mercy on her soul. Or the gods, as she would have put it herself.

The undertaker took my elbow and ushered me towards the black limousine where Cú and Nana were already seated.

I was independent.

At long last.

That night, a knock came to the door.

KNOCK KNOCK KNOCK. Knock.

This happened in the middle of the night, when darkness had fallen even though it was only dark for a few hours at this time of the year. The knock frightened me but I got up anyway. I heard a second knock and then I knew I wasn't dreaming. I looked into Cú's room. He was sleeping like a log.

I went downstairs.

There was a shadowy figure in the porch. I peered through the peephole to get a better look, to see who it was.

Lísín.

The door opened – did I open it? I'm not sure. She stepped into the hall.

Was I frightened? Or shocked? Or even surprised?

In a way. On the other hand, I had known who it was as soon as I heard that knock in my sleep. Lísín's own special knock. Three heavy knocks, then one tiny little knock.

She was dressed as she was when she went on holiday: in her jeans and a pink T-shirt, a little grey hoodie. She wasn't injured in any way.

'Hi,' she said, standing in the middle of the hallway and looking around. 'I'm sorry to drag you out of bed so late at night but I don't know what I did with my key.'

She spoke just as if nothing had happened, as if she were coming home after a night at the theatre or the movies.

She went into the kitchen and sighed.

'OK,' she said. 'Well, well.'

We had tried to tidy it up a bit but now I could see that we hadn't done it very well. Our cleanliness was not up to Lísín's standards.

'OK,' she said, sitting down at the table. 'I'll look after this. The Leaving Cert is starting soon. You'd better get a good night's sleep.'

'Great, good night!' I said quickly. I didn't feel like discussing the Leaving Cert and my plans with Lísín.

But it wasn't so easy to escape.

'You're not thinking of not doing it, are you?'

She stared hard at me. I felt myself blushing.

'Well ...'

'Because that would be ridiculous. It wouldn't be fair to yourself. You've done so much work already. I know things are difficult for you at the moment, but you'll feel a lot better about everything if you face up to the challenge. Putting it on the long finger won't help.'

It made a certain amount of sense.

'But ...' I started. But didn't she know what I was feeling? I missed her and Pól more than I could bear to think of. My world was upside down and I was walking on my head.

'It's two weeks out of your life. Forget about everything else for those two weeks. Then it will be over and you'll be able to do whatever you like.'

She meant, whatever she liked. BESS, she meant. Business studies, or law.

She moved over to the sink and started to fill a bucket.

'I'll take care of the house. You don't bother about any of that till the exams are over. Now go back to bed, you need all the sleep you can get.'

The mop was in her hand, and her face looked calm and happy, just as it always did when she was busy working.

'I love you, Mam,' I said.

Suddenly I was overcome by a wave of tiredness. I had to sleep. I could hardly drag my body back upstairs, and I fell into bed, my legs, my body as heavy as a cold rock.

I hadn't asked Lisín the important questions.

Which were: How did you come back here? Were you killed at all, or injured? Or, Are you a ghost, Mam?

Early in the morning, I woke up. Or, to be honest, I did not wake up. I was woken by the telephone.

But there was nobody on the line when I picked it up.

I looked at the clock. Seven o'clock. It was time to get up, if I was to go to school.

'OK,' I said. 'OK, you're right, Mam, on this occasion.'

I roused Cú. He was taken aback but he got up too. We had breakfast together, just like in the old days, and then we went to the station to catch the train for school.

Everyone was surprised to see me back there. They were kind and inquisitive at the same time. I just said I'd changed my mind. I wanted to do the Leaving after all. It was obvious that some of my classmates thought this was crazy and in bad taste, and others thought it was the sensible thing to do.

In the middle of a maths class the principal called me into her office.

She gave me a big hug and then a cup of tea, which astonished me even more than the hug. They never give us cups of tea in school. That was the first cup of tea I'd been offered there in six years.

'I'm very pleased to see you back with us,' she said. 'And is it true that you want to go ahead and do the Leaving?'

'Yes,' I said. I remembered that neither she nor anyone else knew that my mother was all right, that she was back at home looking after the house and looking after me and Cú. And of course I didn't tell her how things were. It wouldn't be easy to explain. 'I know it'll be tough,' I said. Well, it was always tough, on everyone. 'And maybe I won't do all that well. But if I don't do it now I'll have to wait for a whole year. Is that right?'

'Yes,' she said. 'There's a problem with the system. They don't take into account that accidents can happen, or illnesses. But there's no way around that at the moment.' She looked carefully at me. 'You've made the right decision. You'll be allowed to do the exam in a special room and take some extra time with the papers, if you like.'

This was news to me.

'All right,' I said.

'And I'll set up an appointment with a counsellor for you, so you will have an opportunity to discuss everything. If you would like that, of course?'

'All right,' I said. 'That would be good.' Actually I was getting dizzy, listening to her. I just wanted to get back to the classroom and listen to the teacher talk about algebra. Sitting there in the office, listening to the head nattering on about counsellors and special rooms and all that made me wonder if I was actually out of my mind? Maybe Lísín wasn't home at all, and when I'd go home tonight there'd be nobody there, just the cold, empty, scruffy house.

And so it was. There was nobody at home when we got there that afternoon. But it wasn't scruffy, it was clean and tidy. It looked as if it had been given a good spring cleaning. I could have been mistaken about that though. I don't usually pay much attention to how the house looks. Unless it's a complete kip I wouldn't notice. That's actually a thing Lísín often pointed out about me and Pól and Cú. That we seemed to be blind when it came to the house and dirt and dust and messiness.

Emma dropped by. She was glad to hear we'd gone to school, which was funny: when I said I'd decided to take a break from school and not to do the Leaving, everyone said that I was quite right, that it was sensible. And now when I told them I was doing the opposite, they said exactly the same thing. What did it say about them?

'Now that the funeral is over and everything sort of back to normal, you should try and get back to your usual routines,' she said. This wasn't what she was saying yesterday.

I let it pass. It wasn't the time for arguments. I agreed with her.

'There's to be a meeting with the solicitor at the end of the week, Eileen says. You and your grandmother and him.' She knew more about my life than I did myself. 'Fingers crossed!' She smiled nervously.

'Sure!' I said. Then I asked 'Why? What's with the fingers crossed?'

This question disturbed her, and she started fidgeting with her hands.

'Oh, just that Cú is allowed to stay on living here with you.'

'What else would he do?'

I was getting upset now.

'Ruán, are you feeling OK?' She sounded worried. 'Do you want to lie down or something?'

'I'm all right,' I said. Though I wasn't. I was afraid again.

'What I mean is, I hope they don't make Cú go into some sort of institution or foster care. Or go to live with your gran or some other guardian.'

'My grandmother! She can't take care of herself!'

'Well, that's the problem. But she might be suitable as a legal guardian. Whereas they might not accept you as one because you're so young. But Eileen says the solicitor thinks it will work out. That the two of you will be allowed to stay on here, together. That's what you want, isn't it?'

'Of course,' I said. Jesus, it was complicated.

Emma fixed sandwiches for us. She left all the stuff she used in the preparation all over the kitchen – she wasn't much better at housework than me or Cú, though at least she could cook. Then she went off to get a bit of study in.

✳

In the middle of the night the knock came again. KNOCK KNOCK KNOCK. Knock.

'I'll really have to get a key,' said Lísín. 'I seem to have lost mine. I can't even find my handbag, my good Hermès bag. What has happened to it?'

'I'll try to get you a key,' I said. 'I just have two at the moment, one for me and one for Cú. Eileen and Emma have the others.'

'I hate waking you up like this in the depths of the night. Maybe you could leave your key under the flowerpot in the porch for me?'

'I will,' I said. But actually I knew I wanted to meet Lísín and have a chat with her when she came to the house. Also, I didn't want her to have a key of her own. I wanted to keep track of her. 'I will, if I remember it.' I knew I wouldn't. Even though she was right – it was tiring, getting up at midnight after a long day at school.

She went right into the kitchen and got down to work straight away.

'So, how was school?' she asked as she swept the floor.

'It was fine,' I said. 'I told them I'd do the Leaving. I think they were taken aback but you're right, it's the right decision.'

'Of course it is,' she said. 'And now, back to bed with you, sweetie. And don't forget to put the key under the geraniums tomorrow.'

'I'll try not to forget,' I said.

'You always were a bit of an old scatterbrain,' she said, starting to stack the dishwasher.

I longed to give her a kiss. But something held me back.

14.

CYMRU

COLM

Khallid, my boss, was a decent enough chap once you got to know him. He wasn't the most talkative guy in the world, but then neither am I, so we got along just fine. He had a sense of humour, I'll give him that. I can't recall the witty comments he made about the customers but they popped out of him like newsflashes, all day long.

At first he was always in the shop before me in the morning, and then he'd stay on after I left in the evening. He'd spend about eleven hours in that shop at a stretch. He trained me in, you might say. I didn't really need much training, on account of all my experience in Spar back in Rathbeg. I knew how to operate the till and the checkout and all that. And not to brag, but I knew more about some aspects of shopkeeping than he did. Like I know it's important to keep the place tidy, and I spent the training period attempting to clean up that shop. It wasn't easy. The space was too small for all the stuff he had in it. But I got it into some sort of shape, and it made life easier for everyone.

The place was really busy first thing in the morning, with people on their way to work running in to buy little things – he had newspapers, fruit, biscuits, sweets, sandwiches. All that. Then there'd be a lull until about midday when it would get hectic again with the lunchtime shoppers. The afternoons were in between, people coming in to do normal shopping: bread and milk, veggies. A lot of old people who liked to stay and have a conversation.

I was busy enough and I liked it there. I liked the work and, after a while, as I said, I got very fond of Khallid.

I filled in all the official papers – reluctantly, because I knew it would be easy to trace me once I'd registered my details. But it was funny – after a while in this new town, in this new country, I stopped worrying about what was going on at home. I began to assume that my father was probably still alive and that I wasn't some sort of murderer, and I felt that coming over here had been the right thing to do. Getting away from everything. It was my privilege. If the guards weren't looking for me then I had every right to be over here, working in the shop, doing exactly what I wanted.

Deep inside, I was pretty sure they weren't after me. Because I knew if they were, they'd have caught me by now. I was only seventy or eighty miles from Dublin, when you thought about it. Once this dawned on me I put whatever worries I had left away, in a box stored at the back of my mind, just like I tucked away old umbrellas and lost property in a box at the back of the shop. I had a lost property shop somewhere in the back of my head where those old worries were stored.

But there were times when this didn't work and then I'd be overcome by fear. Petrified. I'd feel certain that my father was dead and the police were hunting me down and I would have to start running, keep running, hide out in London or go abroad to some other country, some terrible place where I could find no work or no friend and be all on my own.

But nothing happened and I just went right on living in Bangor, working in Khallid's shop.

The days slid by.

I spent a week living in the hostel with the red windows, and then I started looking for a flat. When I mentioned to Khallid that I was trying to find a place to live, he had some advice. That's the kind of guy he was: he always had some advice. Quiet as he was, he had his ear to the ground and knew everything that was going on in this town. And everybody. Including a woman who had a room to let for the summer.

The summer.

I'd almost forgotten that I'd said I was a student doing a summer job.

But as it happened there were plenty of places to let for the summer. It was a university town and most of the students had cleared out by now and wouldn't be back until September.

I took the room Khallid knew about. It was in a little house, a bit away from the shop, on the far side of town. There were other rooms to let in the house but they were vacant, so I actually had a whole house to myself for the price of one room.

It wasn't luxurious. No. An old house, probably belonged to a miner or some worker in the old days when there was a lot of coal mining going on in the area around Bangor. Small rooms, basic furniture. A little kitchen containing nothing bar a cooker and fridge. It was smaller than our house at home, but not much, and it had one great advantage: my folks weren't living in it.

I was perfectly happy with it.

Well, happy enough.

I was lonely, I have to admit. When I was at work, everything was hunky-dory – there was plenty to do, I had company. It wasn't long before I got to know the regulars, and some of them loved to stay around and chat. And that is just the sort of company I like. People on the other side of a counter who can't get too close to me.

Then on my way home I'd take some veggies and stuff from the shop and spend a bit of time preparing and eating them.

All the same, I had a fair amount of free time on my own.

It's not that I was used to company. I hadn't many friends back home. Just my mates in the shop and a few guys in school that I wasn't all that close to. I wondered if they'd even notice that I was gone. OK, they'd notice, but would they care?

But at home I was much busier than I was now, over here. At home there was school during the day, and work in the shop at night and at the weekends. In fact I had hardly any time off at all. Now, I was earning more money and I'd more time off than I'd had since I was about fifteen. Leisure time. It was a new one on me and I didn't really know what to do with it.

I went to the pictures about three times a week – then I'd have seen everything that was showing. I've never been into reading, and there was no television in the house. I thought I might buy one sometime, but not yet.

So I decided to look for another job, to use up my spare time and make some extra money. Work was what I knew about; it was all I could do.

I was lucky, again. I've always been lucky when it comes to getting a job; maybe because I've been employed for so long. People like workers with experience.

My new job was in a pub. I'd do that at night and do the day shift in the shop.

Doing both was tough enough. But after a week or so I got used to it. I stopped falling asleep during the day in Khallid's. And the great thing was I was never lonely any more. I hadn't the time. The only time I was at home in my little house I was in bed and fast asleep.

I opened a bank account to save my money. I had to, even though a bank account was another clue to my whereabouts. But my savings started to mount up, especially after I got the second job. I couldn't keep my money under the bed any more.

What was I saving for? A rainy day. The day when I'd be forced to move on.

June was almost over. It had been a good summer so far, and the town looked festive and cheerful. On Fridays – Khallid closed the shop on Fridays, it had something to do with his religion – I went on trips on the train. Llandudno, Preswick, Beaumaris, resorts along the coast of Wales. Beaumaris was the place I liked best. I'd just wander around, enjoying the quaint streets and the great views, eating ice-cream, sitting on the beach. Lots of people were in swimming. I can't swim. I never learnt, even though we're so close to the sea. There was no pool; it's easier to learn to swim in a pool. Come to think about it, there are hardly any swimming pools in Dublin.

Summer.

The Leaving was already over. That thought came to me out of the blue when I was rambling around Beaumaris one Friday at the end of June.

What amazed me was that I hadn't thought of it before. It was such a big deal at home, and here I hadn't even remembered it until now.

I had never been all that interested, let's face it. I did a bit of work at school; I knew I'd pass, or maybe get enough points to get a place in some third level college. That's what one of the teachers told me anyway, even though not many of the kids in my school went on to third level. Most of them passed the exams, a few failed and they all went straight into the workforce and straight out of the educational system and nobody gave a fart as far as I could see.

And I knew that's what would happen to me if I stayed at home; it wouldn't have mattered how good my results were. There wasn't a chance on earth that I'd be able to accept a place in a university or any other sort of college. So what's the point of the Leaving Cert for guys like me? I never got an answer to that question from any schoolteacher. They really wanted us to do it, but I don't think they thought it through properly. None of us were going anywhere where the qualification would count.

I was in the pub the night after I'd been thinking about all this. It was a Saturday night. And somebody from Rathbeg walked into the pub. That girlfriend of Ruán's. The girl he was with at his party. I forgot her name. She was with another girl whom I didn't know. I caught sight of her before she saw me. I think. The pub's kind of dark. She and her pal were chatting and giggling. I managed to avoid them, sliding in behind the bar.

My heart was thumping. In one way I longed to talk to her, to find out. But I was scared shitless.

I pretended to be sick.

'What is it?' The boss glared at me. 'You look as if you've seen a ghost.'

I told him I felt awful.

'OK, just this once.'

I went home, slipping out the back door. All the way home I kept looking over my shoulder, afraid that someone was following me.

15.

MY MOTHER'S SMELL

RUÁN

Lísín visited the house every single night until the Leaving was over. I never left the key outside the door, so I got up every night to let her in and have a chat with her.

I got used to her visits. I'd remain awake until the knock came to the door, always at the same time, just after midnight.

She always wore the same clothes. The jeans and the pink T-shirt she'd worn when she set off on her twentieth-anniversary holiday.

'Would you like to go upstairs and get a change of clothes?' I asked one night, feeling sorry for her. She was such a stickler for clean clothes and now she'd been wearing that T-shirt for more than a month.

But she didn't seem to hear. Or else she just ignored my comment.

She was very interested in the exams. She wanted to see all the papers and she had opinions about all of them. I had to tell her what questions I answered and summarise my responses.

Too challenging, fair, easy-peasy.

I got used to the post-mortems, too. In school they advised you not to do them – everybody did anyway – but I didn't mind them. I didn't mind doing post-mortems with someone who was post-mortem herself!

I knew I was doing fine, even without Lísín's assessments. Every morning I went in and wrote out answers. I felt no nerves whatsoever, much less than I'd ever felt at any other exam. I didn't actually care what result I got. I was doing the Leaving but somehow I knew the outcome wasn't going to affect my life, the way the teachers said it would.

The fact is, even though I didn't know what I'd be doing next, I knew one thing. It wouldn't be business studies. I didn't care what that ghost, my mother the ghost, wanted.

I should say something about Cú. What about Cú? How did he deal with nightly visits from his dead mother?

He didn't have to. He was OK. Most of the time he was on holidays or away at a football camp down the country. That had been arranged before the accident and we stuck to the plan. Counsellors and so on were talking to both of us on a regular basis. Cú seemed to be getting over the whole thing. He's tough. He accepted that Lísín and Pól were gone. He never encountered Lísín on her night visits, and when he was home he never noticed that the house was exceptionally clean and tidy, just as it had been when Lísín was alive. He wouldn't. He never noticed when everything was in a mess, either, because he had other things on his mind. Relating to football, for the most part.

The lawyer had fixed things for us. Cú wasn't going to be living in an institution; he would be allowed to stay at home with me. Some official busybody would call in on us once a week to ensure everything was as it should be. Check that I wasn't abusing Cú in any way and that he was going to school, all that sort of stuff. That I'd remembered to buy food. That he wasn't starving.

This social worker was happy with what she saw.

'Gosh! I'm really impressed!' she gasped, looking around at the house, which was in showroom condition. 'You're a dab hand at the housework. Would you like to come around and do my place when you've got a minute to spare?'

She never stayed longer than about five minutes.

She gave us top marks in her reports. About how spick and span the house was. About how mature and responsible I was. What a great guy. It was true.

Although I was getting a helping hand from the gods, as you might put it.

The final day of the exams – my last was history – Lísín said: 'You've done well. You'll get enough points for your first choice.'

'You could be right,' I said. I knew I wasn't going to accept the place. I'd already filled in the change of mind form, and I'd put down a degree in film studies as my first.

Naturally I wasn't going to reveal this to Lísín.

But somehow she knew anyway.

'I notice you've filled in that change of mind thing,' she said. She was shoving dirty clothes into the washing machine. Her own clothes – those same old jeans etc. – never got dirty, I noticed. No smell. She didn't actually smell of anything, not even her perfume – I still liked to go in and smell that in the big bedroom, like the spirit of Lísín lingering on in the duvet and curtains. A lovely, flowery smell. But it was getting fainter and fainter every day now.

'I have,' I admitted. 'You know I want to do something involving the arts, not business or law.'

'Be sensible,' she said. 'You have responsibilities now. You're looking after Cú. It would make sense to study a subject that would lead to a real career.'

Lísín hadn't filled in any change of mind form, that was for sure, even if she'd changed her status and moved to another dimension. You'd have thought she'd have a new perspective on life from where she was.

'I'll think about it, Mam,' I said, although I thought it was a bit much, her trying to put on the pressure from beyond the grave.

'Promise me you won't post that form,' she said.

'Mam!' I said. 'I love you and I'm really grateful for everything you've done for me, especially since the accident.'

She gave a little smile.

'Don't mention it,' she said. 'I just did what any mother would do.'

'But I can't make that promise.'

The very next day I put the form in the post.

I wasn't going to give in to Lísín now. She was a snob. That's all. She said it was a matter of common sense but I knew it wasn't just that. She wanted to brag about me. That I'd made it into a prestigious course. 'Oh, yes, my son Ruán is going to Trinity College. Business studies.'

She actually believed the angels in heaven would be impressed by the points kids were getting in the Leaving.

That's Lísín!

Next day when I woke up the sun was high in the sky.

I looked at the alarm clock. Ten o'clock. I'd slept through the night without waking once.

I leapt out of bed and raced downstairs. My bag and coat were on the hall floor. Bits of the dinner we'd had the night before were still on the table and the floor was dirty. The heap of clothes I'd left on a chair for Lísín to put in the wash were still there, still dirty.

It was all too obvious that she hadn't paid the house a visit last night. Maybe she'd knocked and I hadn't heard? But that had never happened before. Lísín would keep knocking until someone answered.

No. She must have been sulking because I'd posted that change of mind form. Well, sorry about that, Lísín, but *c'est la vie*.

16.

THUGAMAR FÉIN AN SAMHRADH LINN

EMMA

Me and my friend Rachel were on our way to France to spend a fortnight camping in La Rochelle with Eileen. This was just after the Leaving was over. We invited Ruán to come too but he said no. And I think I know the reason why. He's terrified. Of me. He knows I'm crazy about him. I'm in love with him. But it's not reciprocal. So he thinks I'm going to, like, sexually assault him or something?

So, as a reward, he gets to come in and feed our minging cat at lunchtime.

Ruán's changed lately. Well, that's only to be expected. But it's not that he's despairing or sad or depressed. *Au contraire*. He's more adult and more sensible than he used to be. Much more independent. Plus, he's a freak hausfrau. His place is so perfect you'd swear Lísín was still in business, keeping it up to her *House and Garden* standard, or else that one of those horrible women you see on TV doling out advice on how not to live in a pigsty was coming in on a daily basis, doing the necessary.

Greg's not with us. Yay! He couldn't get leave from the office. That's one great thing about the civil service: they don't get much leave when they're starting off, at Greg's level. He gets twenty days a year or something and he keeps taking odd days off to play golf. He's such a twit. So he hardly ever gets to take a proper holiday.

Eileen's heartbroken, but I'm like, what a pity, no Greg, I'll miss him so much.

Anyway. Rachel and I were going into this pub. We'd stopped in a little town along the route. For some reason we got the ferry in the late afternoon and didn't get into Holyhead till about seven or eight o'clock. So Eileen says, 'Let's stay overnight somewhere in Wales and head on to Southampton in the morning.'

We found a B&B in this little hick town and I said, 'Well, I'm not staying in here all night, let's go out.'

Eileen goes, 'Fine, but we're getting up at 6 a.m. Don't say you weren't warned.'

There was nothing to do in that B&B. We went out.

It was a town like, say, Tralee. Smaller maybe. Not much going on. Scobies with long, messy hair flopping around in tight micro-minis and flip-flops. Like we were. But our legs are not the size of tree trunks.

We went into this pub. And who was the first person I saw? That boy. The guy who used to work in the Spar and who turned up at Ruán's party the day his parents died.

He stayed over that night. I remember that. But I didn't see him after that, or even think of him. So much else was going on.

I go, 'Hey, I know that guy!' to Rachel.

I was just about to go up to him and say hello. But the next thing, he'd vanished.

'What? Where did he go?' I looked around.

'Are you sure it was him?' Rachel said. 'It's dark in here.'

'Sure, I'm sure,' I said. 'I don't know him person-ally, really. But he worked in our local Spar. I saw him all the time. Though, now that I think of it, I haven't seen him there recently.'

'Why don't you ask somebody? Maybe he's just gone in behind the bar or something?'

'It's not important,' I said. 'He might come back. If he doesn't ... he was just a scobie.'

'So, what was he doing at the party then?'

'You know Ruán, he's a communist. Because Lísín was such a terrible snob.'

But the guy didn't come back. We spent an hour in that pub, then moved on to another one. A few fellows chatted us up. Locals, Welsh guys. I liked their accent but they started saying things in their own language which we couldn't understand and we didn't like that so much. So we started saying things in Irish and they said, 'What the hell's that?' So we explained. And they go, 'Hey, cool, you guys have another language too.'

We taught them a few words. Like *póg mo thóin* and the usual useful phrases, and they taught us a few words of Welsh. Then they tried to get us to go on to a nightclub – amazing that there is one in this place – but we said we'd to get up at six in the morning and had to head.

We exchanged mobile numbers.

They were sweet.

I was so tired.

I slept most of the way to Southampton as we drove along the M4 or whatever. Then my phone rang. Ruán.

I told him we were half dead having been out on the piss the night before in Wales.

'Guess what, though?' I said. 'I saw that guy. Cormac. No, Colm. You know, he was at your party. He works in the Spar.'

He whistled.

'What? Where was he?'

'In a pub somewhere in Wales.' I asked Eileen, 'What was the name of that town?'

'Bangor,' she said.

'Bangor.'

'The Jolly Fisherman,' said Rachel.

'The Jolly Fisherman,' I said.

'What did he say?' Ruán sounded anxious.

'Nothing. I didn't get to talk to him. I saw him and the next thing I knew, he was gone. I don't know him anyway.'

'He's been missing for almost two months.'

'What?'

'He ran away from home. He'd some sort of fight with his da, some crap thing. That's why he came to the party. And then he ran away from mine. I didn't think about him; I had other things on my mind, obviously. But Colette next door knows his folks and she was telling me. He hasn't been in touch with his family since he left; they're frantic.'

'So why didn't they put out a missing person thingummy?'

'I don't know,' he said.

'Well, last night he was in The Jolly Fisherman, Bangor. Working there.'

He said, 'I'll tell Colette.'

'So, what was all that about?' asked Eileen when I hung up.

I told the story. She sighed.

'I heard something about that, all right,' she said. 'From Greg.'

'Does Greg know them? This Colm guy and his folks?'

'He knows about them. And from what I've heard Colm is better off in Bangor, if that's where he is.

What age is he?'

'He's, like, the same age as us. Eighteen or so. Gosh, that means he didn't sit the Leaving.'

'Well, I'm not poking my nose into this,' she said. 'The father is a real bad egg, according to Greg.'

Rachel and I made a face. Yuck. Domestic violence and all that crap. It's such a bore.

✳

I phoned Ruán back that night. We were in France, not in La Rochelle, but in some little *pension* on the way down. We'd had a lovely dinner on the bank of a river, wine and all. The weather was warm and beautiful.

'*So* wish you were here,' I said.

'Me too,' he said.

'Hey, did you do anything about Colm of the Spar?'

'Yeah. I rang The Jolly Fisherman. You're right; he's working there.'

'Did you tell his parents?'

'Not yet. I thought I might contact him first, talk to him about it.'

'Eileen says they're not very nice, his folks,' I said. 'She said she's keeping out of the whole thing.'

'I know they're not very nice,' said Ruán. 'I'll think about it. Maybe we should let sleeping dogs lie.'

17.

HAPPINESS

COLM

Life was beautiful.

The two jobs, nicely dovetailed. My new friend, Dafydd. He works in the pub too. I really like him, more than I ever liked anyone back home.

Then this chick from Rathbeg walks into the pub.

I was pretty sure she didn't see me. But how could I be sure? She might have, though the lights are low; you can hardly see the money people give you.

Still, it scared me. If she said a word, they'd be onto me. Even if I wasn't a murderer.

I told Dafydd about it. Not absolutely everything. I told him I'd fled from home and I was afraid they'd be searching for me.

'What age are you?' he asked.

Of course, he was right. I had every right to be wherever I wanted to be. Unless I was wanted for a crime.

'Why don't you call your mum and tell her you're abroad. You don't even have to tell her where you are. Then you'll have nothing to worry about.'

'OK,' I said. 'You're right. I'll do that.'

But I couldn't.

Then, two days later, Ruán walked into the shop.

I was alone. It was the middle of the day. Khallid had gone home for lunch or something. And Ruán marches in. There was no escaping this time. I was behind the checkout.

'Hey, man!' Ruán shook hands with me.

The weird thing is, my eyes filled with tears. I was so bloody glad to see him.

'Hi,' I said. 'So ... It's good to see you.' I couldn't stop crying. 'Are you ... on holiday or what?'

He stopped and let me cry. Luckily there was nobody else in the shop.

'Emma told me she saw you in a pub over here. So I went to the pub and they told me you worked here during the day. What are you up to, man? Your folks are out of their minds with worry.'

My folks. Plural. So my father was still alive.

'The two of them?' I just wanted to be sure.

'As far as I know. From Colette.'

Colette. I'd completely forgotten about her. And little Jacob.

'Is my father all right?'

Ruán shrugged.

'Shouldn't he be?'

'He had a heart attack the day I left Ireland.'

'Well, he must have recovered. Colette saw him yesterday.'

I'd stopped crying now.

'Did you tell Colette I was over here?'

'What do you take me for?' he asked.

I laughed. He was always a good guy, Ruán, even when he was a little chap.

'Hey,' I said, 'I'm finished here about four. Why don't you call by and we'll go for a drink or something?'

I met him at four and we went to a nearby café on the seafront, a nice place.

'A beer?' I offered. It was a very warm day, like most days since I'd come to Wales. I felt the climate was different from the one we had at home, though that could hardly be true.

'I'd prefer a coffee,' he said.

'Likewise.' I ordered two cups.

'Still off the beer?' he asked.

'I don't bother with it. I work in a pub, as you know. For some reason you don't feel like drinking after spending the night working in that atmosphere.'

The coffee came. He gazed out over the water at the island and the bridge that linked the island and the mainland, the Menai Bridge.

'It is beautiful here, all right,' he said. 'So, are you planning on staying?'

At that moment I realised how uncertain I was about everything in my life. I had no plans whatsoever. Until today I'd been on the run from the law, or so I thought. When you're on the run you don't plan for the future; you live from day to day, from hour to hour.

But I wasn't much good at that game, the escape game. Look what I had done. I'd settled down in one place and given my personal information to a lot of people. I knew, as does anyone who ever watched a movie, that that's not the way to escape from anywhere or anyone. A real fugitive keeps moving on all the time. I knew that but I wasn't able to put the theory into practice. I couldn't bear it, to travel incognito, to sleep without a roof over my head, money in the bank. That wasn't for me.

So it was just as well I wasn't a murderer.

'I don't know,' I answered. And I told him everything. Everything except for the bit about Dafydd. The most important bit. I left that out.

Then he told me his story.

Unbelievable.

'I don't listen to the news – there's no television in my house. I think I read something about that bomb in the papers soon after I came here but I didn't pay any attention to it.'

Ruán didn't look as if he was devastated by the tragedy.

'My life has changed completely,' he said. 'I'm lonely; I miss them. They're not around. They don't exist. And what I want more than anything in the world is to be with them again. Just one more time.'

'Well …' I said. And thought, that's impossible.

'It won't happen, ever again.' He stared at me. He seemed to be considering, wondering if he would tell me something more or not. He sighed. 'No, it won't happen. I won't see them again.'

We were silent for a minute and the air was heavy. Then I asked him what he was planning next.

He lightened up. 'I'm going to do a degree in film studies, if I get the points. I did the Leaving.'

After his parents' death, he did it. Wow!

'That's more than I can say,' I said.

'Don't you want to do it?' he asked.

I thought about it.

'Yes,' I said, 'I'd like to. But I'm not sure that it would make much difference to my life. I'd still be working in a shop.'

'You're smart,' said Ruán. 'You could do anything. You know you could. You're one of the smartest people I've ever met.'

I grinned. It's nice to be told you're smart. Not many people had ever said it to me though.

'You could do anything. You should study business or accounting, actuarial studies. You could spend your life as a bigwig manager, a CEO for some giant multinational.'

I laughed.

'I'm not going home,' I said. I knew I would never go back to my father's house.

'I know,' he sighed. 'I get it.'

We watched the sailing boats bounding over the waves like seagulls.

'You won't tell my folks about me, will you?'

I knew the answer but I had to ask.

'No.' He clapped me on the shoulder. 'If you change your mind when the summer is over, give me a call. You're welcome to live in my house, if you want. There's loads of space. You could apply to do the Leaving next year, and then make a decision about the future.'

'Thanks,' I said. I thought about living in that big house on Ashfield Avenue, among those people who usually wouldn't even talk to people like me.

Well, I wasn't about to make a decision right now. I stood up. It was time to go to work in the pub.

'It was great to see you again,' I said. He was my friend. I knew that. The best friend I had when I was in the babies' class in primary school, before either of us understood that I didn't belong in that school, the posh school. Before we both got to understand the class system as it functions in the suburb of Rathbeg, and in Ireland.

'Give me a call now and then,' he said. 'Have you got a mobile?'

I nodded. I'd got one when I met Dafydd, because now I had someone to call and text. Even now I was reluctant to give the number to anyone from home.

But I gave it to Ruán.

'I won't pass it on,' he said. 'Don't worry.' He gave me a hug. 'But why don't you give your mam a call? Just to say you're alive and well. Call from a coin box.'

I said I would. I guessed I probably would, too, in my own time. When I got used to not being a murderer.

I left him sitting at the table, looking at the Menai Bridge. He looked very alone, and sad, even though he was brave and tough.

I was more sorry for him than I could say.

But my own heart was light as I walked towards The Jolly Fisherman. I was as happy as I had ever been in my entire life.

18.

THE THIRD KNOCK

EMMA

We'd a really great trip. Sun, sand, sea. Dancing. A couple of old ruins to give a cultural tinge to the whole enterprise and keep Eileen happy.

Greg was at home when we got back. I'd known he would be, but it bothered me all the same. We didn't even get to open our own door – he opened it for us. Anyone would think he owned the place, not Eileen.

'See ya!' I said, instead of, 'Hello, lovely to be back, dearest Greg.' That shook him.

I went over to Ruán's. He just gave me a big long kiss. Like, what is going on here?

'Are you … OK?' I asked, when I got a chance, after five minutes.

'I'm really glad you're home,' he said. 'I missed you like anything.'

'Could you repeat that?' I asked.

'I missed you like anything.'

And he gave me another long kiss.

Someone knocked on the door while we were kissing.

KNOCK KNOCK KNOCK. Knock.

I looked over my shoulder and thought I saw a shadow at the window.

'Hey!' I said. 'Is there someone at the door?'

He listened. Knock. Knock. Knock. Fainter this time.

'Nah,' he said, hugging me again. 'It's nothing but the wind.'